A TIME
that stops the meaningless whirl of the days
and makes each moment infinitely precious

A PLACE
far removed from the world and all of its lies

A LOVE
that strips away all barriers between a man
and a woman—and shows them as they really are
to each other and to themselves

If it happens even just once in a lifetime,
you can count yourself lucky . . .

THE CLEARING
you will never want to leave it.

The Clearing
by Thérèse de Saint Phalle

Translated by Eileen Finletter

POPULAR LIBRARY • NEW YORK

Published by Popular Library, a unit of CBS
Publications, the Consumer Publishing Division
of CBS Inc.

June, 1978

ISBN: 0-445-04234-6

Original title in French: *La Clairière*

PRINTED IN THE UNITED STATES OF AMERICA

For Julien Gracq,
who told me about Sweden.

The critical moment in the life of a man
is that moment in which he decides to face death.

Che Guevara.

I

It seemed to him that he had crossed countless forests, his passage through them symbolizing the essential nature of his life. He could no longer remember when he had not been making his way in darkness through a lattice of almost contiguous tree trunks beneath a canopy of leaves. He walked deep into the moldy underbrush, stumbling over roots and shuddering at the grotesque sensation of trampling upon rotting corpses. With every step he took, a whiff of the sickeningly sweet odor of decay rose from the lush undergrowth of vegetation. Total silence—a silence that had existed from time immemorial, an experience of Siberian isolation—surrounded him. Not a leaf stirred, no breeze quickened the branches of the stark, stiff trees standing perfectly still, waiting for the first breath of air.

Pierre pushed blindly ahead, forced to continue on

if he were to avoid being dragged down into a swamp which would have swallowed him completely. Desperately fatigued, he tried to control his breathing and movements in order to save what little strength was left him. His joints and the small of his back ached incessantly, his legs were weighted down with irons, he was functioning like a robot. Though he longed to lie at the foot of a giant Sequoia and never rise again, the instinct for self-preservation impelled him along the trail. The lordly, oppressive forest, a survival from a tertiary age that had eliminated all life extraneous to its own vitality, terrified him. As he pressed on into the hostile, dense, impenetrable labyrinth, he had the impression that he was slowly sinking deep into the heart of the great Pacific.

Like a fish gazing up from the bottom of the sea, he caught sight of rays flashing, as indistinct as reflections glimpsed in the blue-green depths of an ocean. Little by little the foliage became more distinct. Light showed between the columns of tree trunks, which seemed to spread apart now, freeing the long-haired moss, rippling like seaweed; clusters of shimmering shrubs dotted with berries became visible. The hum of insects buzzing arose from the twigs and branches. A bird's cry echoed through the air. Pierre realized that day was drawing near; his voyage without dawn or dusk was reaching its end.

The sky turned pale, and the sudden glare dazzled his eyes. Shading them with one hand, he staggered onto a sandy heath strewn with scraggy scrub. His arms folded, he fell, abandoning himself to his body's pain and to the warmth of the sand beneath him. When he opened his eyes, he saw a sparkling lake with a strange phantasmagoria in its center—an island, on which there arose wooden houses and churches whose golden towers were reflected in the water along the banks of the river. Dovecotes and windmills dotted the landscape. He glimpsed lacings of stone, spires rising out of domes, clusters of pillars linked by incurving cornices, a fortress conceived by a creator drunk with beauty, who had offered up to God an unknown masterpiece.

Pierre stood up, determined to find a small boat so as to reach the beach and approach the citadel now clearly outlined against the morning sky. No woman participated in this adventure. Leonore least of all.

His muscles contracted and he awakened. Not far from him, seated before a bridge table, Leonore was smoking as she wrote in a notebook some phrases from a manual for use in the class she was to teach the following day. He detested her dressing gown, dotted with orange and red poppies and faced with black satin.

"Did you have a good sleep?" she asked.

She had probably watched him closely as he slept, like a praying mantis, obsessed as she was with the desire to devour him while he lay at the mercy of her claws. She was surely capable of swallowing him up completely. How had he let himself be caught in such a trap?

Pierre got out of bed, collected his clothes, and went into the bathroom, locking the door behind him. Already thirty years old! The mirror reflected his gaunt face, with hazel eyes that turned reddish brown when he was angry or indignant. He had never become accustomed to his looks, which resembled those of a wolf eaten up by some secret despair.

"Are you hungry?" Leonore cried through the door.

She had spent three years weaving the net with which she meant to capture him. Let her try! No one was going to move into his two-room refuge. His books, reaching from floor to ceiling, protected him from the world outside. A camp bed, a desk, several chairs, including an early nineteenth-century armchair, a small kitchen, and a bathroom sufficed to fill his needs. His mother, who invaded this sanctuary twice a year, reproached him for this. She curled up in the easy chair, tossed her dyed blond curls, and cried:

"My poor darling! How can you live in such a ridiculous apartment? Do you want some money so that you can move?"

Her hair was short, her shoulders were smooth, and she adored luxury: Her second husband's income made it possible for her to pay for a gerontologist who stuffed her with vitamins and hormones. Her skin was fresh, her body that of a model's, thanks to hours spent at beauty parlors and health spas. She dressed in handsome sport clothes of soft suede and cashmere, her jewels were signed *Cartier*.

"How old are you, Mama?" he inquired.

It was amusing to watch her manipulate the truth, change the subject of conversation with ease and charm.

"When are you coming to visit us in Virginia? We own six horses now."

"And a tennis court, rhododendrons which date from the War Between the States, four gardeners, priceless silver and china, three thousand bottles in the wine cellar, a penthouse apartment in New York whose terraces offer a marvelous view of Manhattan, including the Hudson River and the Atlantic Ocean. Your inventory doesn't interest me!"

Vera sighed, losing not a spark of the gaiety illuminating her face. If her American husband should suffer a heart attack, she would immediately find another. Pierre suspected that she had even gone so far as to have several candidates whom she was holding in reserve for such an eventuality. Why didn't he have a normal mother who was plump, wore her gray hair in a chignon, and enjoyed preparing a delicious beef stew?

Leonore shook the door handle impatiently.

"Did you hear me? Do you want some dinner?"

"No, I have some work to finish up. I must go home."

A torrent of reproaches penetrated into the bathroom. While dressing, Pierre congratulated himself on having escaped from such a possessive woman, whose one desire was to hold him captive in her clutches. He was satisfied to see her only once a week. Passively subservient to a habit that he did not have the courage to break off, he also believed that he belonged to a different generation from that of the chic, attractive girls he ran across in the corridors of the television studios where, in his capacity as literary critic for a daily newspaper, he participated in a literary program. He could easily have struck up an acquaintance with any one of them, but he had no talent for seduction. He did not relish the prospect of putting on an act, and he was too timid simply to be natural.

Leonore sulked. The unmade bed with its rumpled sheets bore witness to an intimacy between them that Pierre had already forgotten. She probed, trying to reach the innermost recesses of his heart and soul, as a searchlight might explore the crevices of a rocky coast.

Sheer laziness kept him tied to her. He feared the complications of approaching another woman, beginning a new affair. He lived in relative isolation. His two novels had not made much of a ripple. Who would pay attention to him for three hundred pages? His companions at the studio were too busy jockeying for position in the hierarchy and trying to catch the eye of those in power in order to present their own projects. His editor published thirty books a month. His journalist friends were preoccupied by the political gossip and love affairs of the Parisian social set. Who was really concerned about Pierre? His mother was delighted to be living in the United States, where she received senators at her estate in the South, her house celebrated for the luxurious refinement of its interior, the extraordinary dinner parties that took place there. She reveled in the descriptions of her receptions, published in the local newspapers. Luckily, she had no other children.

Leonore's unflagging passion wore him out and made him uneasy. He had refused to show her his grandparents' house in the country, which he had inherited, nor had he ever permitted her to spend the night in his apartment. He thought it best to be circumspect, and so kept their social activities down to a minimum—an occasional dinner at a restaurant, an evening at the cinema, once in a while an art exhibit. He had once owned a cat named Tatate. Sitting on his lap, its ears laid back, the animal had only one idea—to jump and run away. But it dissimulated such a desire for independence under the pretence of sleep, until the moment when Pierre's grasp would loosen and it could easily make its escape. Leonore revealed the same patience as the cat, never losing sight of her final objective.

"See you soon!" she said.

"I'll call," he replied.

He felt relieved the moment he left her, happy to idle away his time sauntering about the streets, his hands in his pockets, free, free, free.

Leonore's brown eyes flashed a reproach shining like a barrage of insults. Pierre leaned over and lightly kissed her on the forehead.

"What are you doing next week?" she inquired.

He raised his eyebrows and absently replied:

"I've been invited to Sweden to give two lectures, one in Stockholm, the other in Kiruna, near the polar circle."

Leonore pushed away the table so sharply that her books slipped to the floor.

"To Sweden! But you never mentioned it to me!"

"Must I tell you everything I plan to do?"

Her breathing became rapid, her breasts rose and fell as her temper came to a boil:

"You're being exceedingly unpleasant! When I think of everything I've done for you!"

He sensed an impossible scene in the offing.

"Let me verify the dates. I'll call you. Good night, Leonore."

Pierre ran out, slammed the door behind him, then rushed down the stairs as though fleeing from the Furies who might somehow be following him.

Above the clouds that hovered over the rooftops, swept by the April wind, he caught sight of a fixed star, the same star that he had gazed at above the fir trees, seeking consolation, when, as a child, he had been obliged to go up to bed alone, before the adults. It reassured him, though he could not understand why that should be so.

II

"Aren't you tired?"

At the home of a married couple, professors who presided over the Cultural Association of Kiruna, the evening was ending. About forty people, half of them students, were crowded into the three-room apartment, drinking beer and nibbling at *sill* (the national fish), smoked eel, and other hors d'oeuvres. Pierre was relaxed and talkative, happy to join in these conversations, whose vivacity surprised him. In Paris, literary dialogue was rare indeed. Here, the pale wood walls and the bookshelves stuffed with books and brightly colored sculpted wooden animals seemed to encourage discussions in which people not only asked many questions but had a real interest in the answers. "How long does it take you to write a book?" "Do you accumulate your material for a book ahead of time?" "Do you write by hand or do you use a

15

typewriter?" "Are your plots based on fact; are your characters inspired by real people you've known?"

He had been surprised when his hosts had immediately recognized him at the railway station, until they explained that his photograph had appeared in the newspaper along with an announcement of the lecture date.

Kiruna was thirteen hundred kilometers to the north of Stockholm. Through his compartment window, Pierre had observed the fields buried under white down; chalets, barely perceptible behind a vortex of white snowflakes, resembling a Chagall in the pale bluish light; the birch forests, dotted with frozen ponds; the leaden pallor of the sky; the archipelago where swarms of gulls were wheeling to and fro. At the railway stations, children, warmly muffled in colorful anoraks, their cheeks a glowing apple-red, held hands as they stood patiently waiting for the train; their parents had the wind-bitten faces of people who go outdoors in all weather; most of them had the bright blue eyes of northern peoples.

The couple were in their mid-forties and quite handsome. He had clear-cut features, his face was burned a ruddy reddish brown from the inclement weather of the north; she had high cheekbones, her eyes were large and slightly slanted. As they led him to their car, they thanked him for having made such a long trip. They had organized a group which met from time to time to discuss contemporary works of literature, paying writers of their choice to come, often from very far away, to meet with them. Madame Selsviken taught art history, her husband literature. Pierre had once before felt the same sensation of instant communication, when his Japanese editor had invited him to Tokyo to launch his first novel. There too he had been struck by the immediate contact with his public, despite the fact that he and they belonged to such disparate civilizations. They were united in their passion for literature, moved by the great works of Russian writers, the new American novelists, the romantic Germans. Returning from Japan, Pierre was certain that he had found there a true "meeting of the minds." And at Kiruna that impression occurred once again.

As he ate the cold hors d'oeuvres—shrimp, salmon, slices of reindeer meat, white cheese smothered in paprika, a mixture of raw vegetables, amidst people who knew not only his own books but the works published that year by other French writers, he was persuaded that together they formed a true community. He realized that when he was abroad the ugly duckling became a swan, taking part in a group and sharing with others. It was so rare to be able to live in harmony with himself as part of a collective spirit, to share an identity with others without aggressiveness or competitiveness! In Paris, the writers he admired kept aloof: they traveled or took refuge in their homes in the country. Literary discussions were virtually nonexistent; the patrons and their salons were fast disappearing. When Pierre had published his second novel, he had received about three hundred letters and had been surprised to see that the bottle he had tossed into the sea had reached port. Apart from this mail, he had no relations with his readers. His shyness, his lack of talent for establishing contacts, his work that permitted him to earn his living without being obliged to keep regular office hours, the existence of Leonore, only reinforced his isolation. He felt more lost in the rue Mazarine where he lived than abroad in a foreign country, faced with an alien culture.

Dorotea, the Selsvikens' daughter, was studying the Laplanders civilization and the Lapp language at the university. She reacted violently against their segregation, denounced the dislocation of their way of life by the West with its transistor radios and its tourists who were contaminating the Lapp civilization and fast destroying it. She had her mother's large eyes, flowing blond hair, and a lively personality. Her friends, both male and female, dressed in velours trousers and Shetland sweaters, were clear-eyed, with healthy white teeth, slapped each other on the back, embraced with gusto at the drop of a hat. They criticized the preceding generation, whom they considered to be obsessed with professional advancement and the accumulation of material riches.

"Aren't you going to defend yourselves?" he inquired of Madame Selsviken, who was passing around a plate of sandwiches.

"We respect everyone's opinions, including those of our children," she replied.

"And you, Dorotea?"

The young girl tossed her head:

"We don't respect our parents simply because they have conceived us, sometimes accidentally. They must earn our good opinion of them. Age carries no special privileges in our eyes. *Skol!*"

With one gulp she emptied her glass. Three young men came up to Pierre and asked him about his political position. He was embarrassed to say that he held aloof from such preoccupations. The young Swedes admired their liberal and dynamic prime minister, who was gifted with great magnetism. They were shocked by the idea of aggression, hated war and violence, and believed that each individual was free to dispose of his own life as he saw fit. The suicide rate in Sweden each year reached the same number as those victims of a medium-sized war during the nineteenth century.

Erik, Dorotea's boyfriend, challenged him with a question:

"Is it thinkable that ultra-secret laboratories in the United States, in the Soviet Union, and in China are cultivating and stocking supplies of viruses capable of annihilating or disabling millions of human beings?"

One of his comrades heatedly continued:

"We're for the establishment of a world government that will oblige all countries to completely disarm. Besides the five nations that belong to the atomic club, about a dozen countries have reached the technological level necessary for production of the bomb—Sweden, Japan, Australia, the Republic of West Germany, India, Brazil, Argentina, among others. Israel already possesses an atomic weapon. Any one of them could reduce New York City to ashes within several minutes. Just think of an anonymous war waged by teleguided missiles or satellites equipped with a nuclear warhead! It would be impossible to know the identity of the guilty party! Our strength lies in our youth. We're certain to win out over the nationalists and the warmongers. They'll die before us, after all!"

At ten o'clock Pierre decided that he really did need to go to bed. He wanted to go over the talk he would be giving the next day. He had drunk more than usual, seduced by the Swedish *akvavit* with its taste of anise and caraway, a drink that helped the

Swedes to disregard the toll of the interminable frozen winter months. An architect and his wife offered to drop him at his hotel. The car slid along as silently as a sleigh through a landscape belonging to another planet. Pierre was happy to reach his cozy room with its walls of russet-brown latticework, a pine table, a comfortable bed covered with a handwoven quilt, a lamp shaped from a wooden hammer, probably sculpted by a woodcutter during a long winter's night. After a hot bath he slipped into bed, his head swimming as a result of the voyage and the four hours of conversation.

Some of his colleagues had told him that they gave their lectures extemporaneously, improvising as they went along. Pierre could not do that, however. He was obliged to write about twenty pages, then revise them, underlining the most important passages before memorizing his speech. What miracle had made it possible for him to publish two novels? The first chapters of the third were in his suitcase. Would he ever finish it? Each time he sat down to write, the same anguish seized him. The cabinetmaker knows whether the armchair he is making is properly balanced; he can judge its curves and proportions because he is an expert. But the writer probes the innermost recesses of his being, sounding the voices deep within him so as to extract each word, one after the other; his characters originate from a mysterious depth that the writer himself is incapable of truly understanding. While the process continues, it is impossible for him to know if his work is of any real value.

Pierre had chosen the myth of the "double" for his theme. A man is traveling abroad and meets a second self, that person whom he might have become if a twist of fate had not changed his course. If it had not been for the war and the death of his father, Vera would have raised several children instead of running as a couturier's representative from country to country looking for clients. Her son would not have been sent to boarding school, where he had sought refuge in his imagination like all those who suffer from loneliness. Contented and easygoing, he might have become an engineer, married, had children. It is possible that he would have run a business, frequently taking a plane to faraway countries to acquire contracts for his company. Flying over Labrador to reach the United States, perhaps he would have gazed at a trail running along the forest and leading to a small isolated house on the edge of a lake. He might have tried to imagine the life of the fur trapper who lived there, unaware that he was proposing the same questions as a novelist. Would he have regretted having smothered his literary talent? If it had not been for the solitude of his youth, perhaps he would have led the same life as everyone else. Prisoner of his career, he would not have been able to break out of the confines he had created for himself. If he had stayed the night in Kiruna, it would have been merely to visit the iron-ore mines.

Pierre put the text of his talk on the bedside table and turned out the light. No bird, no distant murmur broke the silence. While driving home, he had been astonished by the quiet, empty streets, ghostly in the pale light of dawn. No dog prowled, no cat disappeared around the corner of a wall. Snow-encrusted birch trees bordered the sidewalks; the houses seemed to shiver under a whitish fog that threatened to insinuate itself inside their walls. Shovels were left planted in a pyramid of hardened snow beside the porches. Seagulls, their wings widespread, stalled above, looking crucified against the milky sky. Everyone remained snugly cloistered within his home, and through the unshuttered windows, shadows could be seen silhouetted against the lighted background: a child bent over a table, its mother with a bowl in her hand, a man reading his paper, a young girl brushing her hair. Sudden snapshots with which Pierre identified himself for the space of a second.

Feeling drowsy from the warmth of the eiderdown, he imagined himself living in one of those houses. He would have given courses at the university during the day, returning home in the late afternoon. His German shepherd dog would have almost thrown him down when it leapt to greet him. Dorotea, busy preparing sandwiches and wearing a red-flowered apron, would throw her arms around his neck. The baby would smile up at him as it crawled over the linoleum floor. At the end of the week, they would ski forty kilometers a day down the reindeer trails, sleeping in shelters, sharing the dried meat of the forest rangers, drinking akvavit straight from a fur-covered flask. The still cascades, the frozen lakes, the ice-covered streams, the sea, glacified into a single block of crystal, would have given them the sensation of becoming petrified, turning into stone themselves.

In the depths of his slumber, Pierre heard muffled booms reverberating in succession, the echoes resounding in a crescendo. A cannon thunders in just that way, with a continuous rumble that increases until it becomes a powerful roar. He realized that he was not dreaming—a confused, distant murmur was coming from the neighboring forest, all of whose branches seemed to be cracking at the same time. He threw back the covers and rushed to the casement window. The moonlight, shining down on the rooftop opposite, burnished the church tower and turned the horizon beyond the town a dusty white. Someone was running down the corridor. Pierre opened his door and saw a hotel servant, her hair undone, dressed in bathrobe and slippers, scurrying towards the staircase. He asked what was happening. She smiled and replied:

"Oh, sir, it's the great thaw! The first sign of spring. Finally! Winter ends on the night of April thirtieth. The frost has broken and the ice is melting. I must rush off to make sure that the ducks haven't escaped from their hutch."

She disappeared in a flash. Pierre returned to his room, but he had lost any desire to sleep. He was curious to see the great event at first hand. He dressed in long woolen underwear and a ski outfit that he had had the foresight to buy in Stockholm, and also put on a close-fitting cap that covered his ears, as well as fleece-lined leather gloves. The lobby was empty; he kept his key in his pocket and went outdoors. He shivered, his face smarting from the cold of the night. The stars twinkled more brilliantly than usual, as though trying to light his way.

Pierre walked quickly through the dark, deserted streets. Within ten minutes he had reached the last houses at the end of town. The snow, frozen solid, crackled under his boots. The first trees, veiled in white, appeared as a foretaste of the forest beyond them. Birches and fir trees, smothered in a white blanket, standing clear against the black curtain of night, enveloped him with their silent presence. Only the sound of his footsteps on the frozen ground and the occasional fall of dead wood disturbed the stillness around him. He pressed on into the heart of the forest, searching for some sign of life in the midst of the glacial hush, but he heard only the echo of his own footsteps. He stopped to catch his breath. What had prompted him to leave his warm bed at such an hour in search of the first sign of spring? Life ought to have taught him to be on guard against such wild impulses. While he was preparing for his degree in literature, he had lent his notes to a fellow student, a German girl, who had missed some classes. He had fallen into the habit of accompanying her to her home, walking along the banks of the Seine, stopping to browse at the booksellers' stalls. He had been moved by Frederica's gray eyes, her blond pigtails, her awkwardness, her innocence. They had embraced in the shadow of Notre Dame, sitting on a stone stair under the willow tree at the tip of the Île de la Cité to gaze at the reflections dancing on the water from the lights of the Pont-Neuf bridge. With Frederica he discovered García Lorca, Rilke, Proust, and Love. Lying in his arms, she recited the poems of Hölderlin and of Goethe, stanzas he interrupted with his kisses. Farther on, a young boy played the guitar. Pierre's passion for Frederica led him into the heart of a sensitive, tender world of feeling and emotion in which music, painting, poetry, the quality of the play of light on the leaves of the poplars, filled him with ardent delight. It was a blessed spring, a miraculous year! Then the school term had come to a close and Frederica had returned to Germany to spend her vacation with her parents. She and Pierre wrote to each other daily. Pierre had no notion that Frederica's father might not be pleased to hear that his daughter hoped to marry a penniless student. But in the fall the industrialist sent her to a university in California. Her letters became scarce, then stopped completely. The following year she married an American engineer. This initiation with Frederica into a secret harmony underlying the apparently chaotic world, a harmony based on charm, grace, love, and beauty, had remained with him down through the years.

He walked along the edge of a torrent in which blocks of ice resembling huge dice were colliding, the reverberation reminiscent of the clashing of cymbals during an allegro movement. The turbulent waters could be glimpsed between the ice floes as they swelled with life, impatient to throw off the white carapace that had encased them in a prison throughout the devastating winter. Crocuses were beginning to sprout through the snow, ready to burst into bloom at the first encouraging waft of a warm breeze.

"Fiskar ni laxforeller så här dags?"

Leaning against the trunk of a fir tree, a silhouette, muffled up in a fur-collared raincoat, stood out against the background of light and shade. The man repeated the phrase, then, realizing that Pierre did not understand, asked him in English what country he came from.

"France."

The stranger spoke again, in imperceptibly accented French:

"I was asking if you were trout fishing at this hour."

"I wanted to get a close look at the end of the long freeze," Pierre shouted.

"I can barely hear you! Try to join me," the man replied.

The torrent was too wide to be crossed in one jump. Pierre tested the steep bank with his foot to insure that it would not give way under his weight. Leaping several times from one block of ice to another, he reached the other side. The stranger held out his hand to pull him ashore. He was a big, lean, broad-shouldered, limber man who seemed to be about thirty-five years of age.

"It's not very warm. Would you like to continue our conversation in my car? It's parked not far from here."

"That sounds like a fine idea!"

They plunged into the woods, plowing ahead under branches bowed beneath the weight of huge piles of snow.

"Do you live in Kiruna?" Perrre asked.

"No, in Stockholm."

The Swede moved with that elusive look of style that some athletes achieve, majestically, like a wild beast who does not deign to watch for the traps set to catch him.

A Bentley was parked at the edge of a clearing, at the center of which towered a giant oak. To the left stood a huge stone slab on which were traced the footprints of birds and squirrels.

"What are you doing here, may I ask?"

"The Cultural Association of Kiruna invited me to give a lecture."

"Ah, an artist!"

"A writer."

"Well then, you must appreciate stories. Perhaps you would be interested to learn that you are standing in one of those sacred clearings of the Hyperboreans. People coming from the forests of the North Pole invented in such places the cult of divine fire and prayed to the sun as the holy spirit."

The branches of the tree rustled while Pierre listened to his companion describe a woman, her hair falling loose, who, under the light of the moon, inspired by visions from the past, evoked the souls of ancestors with incantations chanted in unison by her audience, accompanied by the moaning of the wind.

"After the glacial era and life in the caverns, a yearning for light and a boundless desire to be delivered from darkness haunted human beings. About seven thousand years ago, the hunters from Perigord followed the herds of reindeer which migrated toward the northern part of Europe. They settled in the forests, from the Atlantic to the polar regions."

The Swede went up to the stone slab and scratched the snow with his fur glove. Some moss appeared on the weatherbeaten surface.

"Our ancestors erected menhirs such as this. Their druid priests practised magic rites that had been used before them by the sorcerers of prehistoric times, who passed them on to their disciples during a long initiation period. They worshipped the sun goddess, to whom they offered human sacrifices—on this slab here, for example."

He smiled.

"The night of the great thaw, summer bursts upon us, putting an end to our misery, freeing us from our primordial fear, lighting the shadows of the night. This change in the seasonal cycle is taking place tonight! Fire which protects and purifies is lit on the hills, in the woods, in the fields, in the towns and courtyards, to chase away the winter. The old women will burn herbs in receptacles used only for this purpose, and the lost, the ill-loved, the mad, and the unlucky become supremely lucid and see clearly enough to understand the truth about themselves. The cards are reshuffled; there's a new distribution."

His breath quickened, he seemed caught in a dream.

"We celebrate the return of spring with songs and dances that reach back to the origins of time itself."

He pointed to the stone slab.

"Look at this menhir, visited only by animals and birds today. You and I are the first pilgrims to come to it in several thousand years. Things happen differently in Sweden than elsewhere. We have never lost sight of our beginnings. The Celts, the Scythians, the Indo-Europeans, all represent subdivisions of a single primitive family branch whose direct descendants settled down here and never left—us! Though the human mind itself has not changed in the past hundred or two hundred thousand years, Homo sapiens accomplished its cultural revolution thirty-five thousand years ago. This belief, this celebration with its symbols and its rites, has endured since that time, and we are the last to have conserved it."

He suddenly came back to the present.

"Please excuse me. Here I've been describing the history of this clearing for you, and you must be dying of the cold!"

"No. I'm warmly enough dressed."

Pierre was delighted with his adventure, his curiosity highly stimulated.

"I've finished correcting my lecture. If I have some lapses of memory tomorrow, so much the worse for the reputation of French writers! For the moment I have no desire to sleep. This is my first visit to your country, and it fascinates me."

The stranger smiled.

"Please allow me to tell you only my first name—Bernt."

He paced back and forth before the menhir, then said:

"I have a hunting lodge several kilometers from here. Would you accompany me there?"

Pierre was to attend a lunch given in his honor by the cultural society. Until then, his time was his own. They turned to the Bentley. Bernt suddenly looked extremely tired. Under his fur-lined raincoat he was wearing a suit made in London's Savile Row. His hands, slim and tapering but firm as those of a pianist, held the steering wheel in their strong grasp. They started to drive through the forest.

"The collective soul of our ancestors still troubles us. We've become industrialized, but we haven't lost our faculty for communicating with the invisible. We threw ourselves full force into the modern era to escape from our ties with the past. We became pioneers of the future in order to liberate ourselves from that past. But high salaries, equality between men and women, free abortions, contraception, have not cured our spiritual disquiet."

Bernt accelerated. The woods thinned out as the road became more passable for vehicles.

"We are gambling on the future. Thirty percent of our citizens possess atomic shelters, and still something is lacking!"

Pierre wondered what was causing this excitement, this vehemence in Bernt. The latter continued, as though the icy solitude which had been confining him had finally cracked.

"Our education prepares us for action rather than for intellectual speculation. We have thrust aside the old dream, although we still believe in magic, in omens, and feel the need of mystical experience. Jobs, acquired skills, are within everyone's reach; we have comfortable apartments, automobiles, incorruptible civil servants; our schools, our professional training have made us rate among the best technicians in the world. But to what end? The law guarantees a paradise—from which we have chased our gods. Nevertheless, they still exist!"

"But the Swedish people enjoy the highest standard of living in Europe!" Pierre interjected.

"Yes, our people have been literate for over a century. Our social revolution took place peacefully; we have not taken up arms since 1814. But here we are today, lame, deaf, mute, because we have forgotten our ancient rites, the eternal sacred mysteries."

Bernt fell silent, concentrating on the road. The car reached an intersection branching off in several directions, the roads fairylands bordered with fir and birch trees, their branches blanketed in snow. He turned to Pierre.

"Do you often devote your time to strangers?"

"I'm a peculiar duck. Nothing interests me more than to understand a fellow human being. Are you married?"

"Yes, and my wife is perfect. We have three children. They have cast me into a role and assume that I will play it. If I were to allow the mask to slip, showing my true colors, I'm not at all sure that my family would approve. It might well lead to a nasty shock if I did not present to the world the image they have invented."

The car, which by now had reached the main road, was headed east. Bernt noticed that Pierre was looking at him questioningly.

"Don't worry. We'll soon reach a side road leading to my lodge. I've just spent two days there completely alone. I almost died of it!" Bernt shrugged his shoulders. "There are days when life becomes truly insupportable. Our friends who come to dine are as virtuous as we. Everyone plays his role as though on stage, so as to fulfill the tribal rites of our social set. We make sure to have a well-balanced invitation list—a cabinet minister, a journalist, a businessman, a lawyer, whose wives assure their public relations and conduct their publicity campaigns for them in the social arena. When these people are drinking, eating, exchanging flattering compliments, I see them as they really are—stripped of the conventions that serve as their crutches. They accumulate privileges (high salaries, titles, decorations, yachts) so as to escape their obsession—the passage of time, the fact that they are growing old. They try to win the race against the others when, in reality, the sole victor is death. Each one gorges himself with illusions in the hope of escaping the day when he must finally settle his account. That is why I get drunk on vodka. No one is ever aware of this except my wife, who then puts me to bed."

Bernt appeared to have crossed over the frontier of a trip to a country peopled with ghosts, a land of shadows. Though they had barely met, Pierre felt a surge of tenderness for him. He had the impression that he was helping a truly lost man, a derelict. His eyes fixed on the horizon, Bernt accelerated on the narrow road winding between the trunks of the fir trees. He seemed in haste to find shelter and protection within his familiar walls.

III

A HUGE MANSION, SHAPED LIKE A STONE CUBE, WHICH would have seemed imposing in any rich residential quarter, looked absurd in the middle of a clearing that had been converted into a park bordered with snow-covered fir trees.

"It's unbelievable!" exclaimed Pierre. "How did an architect ever dream up such a pavilion in the middle of the forest? What a job it must have been to bring the stones all this distance!"

"The marble is from Carrara, in Italy. Of course I realize that it's ridiculous," replied Bernt as he opened the car door and stepped into the snow, gleaming white in the moonlight.

He unlocked the door to the house, and continued:

"My grandfather liked to indulge his fancies. Instead of constructing the usual log chalet, using the trunks of trees growing in the vicinity, he preferred to build this Trianon where he and his friends stayed while they hunted reindeer."

A large-antlered moose head, whose glassy eyes stared at stuffed deer heads, imperiously looked down on the entrance hall, its floor laid with red and black checkered tiles. They entered the drawing room, whose drawn velvet curtains covered the windows completely. The thick vermilion carpet, the soft brown plush sofa, the shotguns hanging on a Spanish leather panel, the white bearskins, mouths open as though ready to swallow their prey, the bookcases and the wood-paneled walls radiated luxury. Pierre followed Bernt into the dining room, its walls set in natural wood, its furniture made of comfortable English leather. In the red-lacquered kitchen with its polished steel sinks, and its ultramodern built-in appliances, there was an Italian coffeemaker identical to those found in Roman cafés.

Bernt opened the refrigerator.

"I like to spend some time here alone. It's the only place where I can recuperate. During the week I delegate as much responsibility as I can to my associates, but the final decisions are mine. The most important clients will deal only with the president."

Boxes of precooked dishes were lined up on platters. Bernt piled four bottles of beer and some sandwiches onto a tray. This he put on the low table in the drawing room and proceeded to divide up the sandwiches on two plates.

"We own part of the forest, we have wood-pulp factories, we export prefabricated houses, we possess four banks, which in turn control a group of companies. Before his death, my grandfather named me his successor."

Pierre swallowed a morsel of smoked reindeer and drank some beer, enjoying its delicious aftertaste of wild honey. He suspected that Bernt was an exceedingly strange man. The latter explained his business methods.

"We must push hard for a yearly increase of ten percent in our companies' earnings. It would be fatal if we were to slow down or come to a standstill. It is indispensable that executives be chosen wisely, that they be given discretionary powers to act. It is my responsibility to create an *esprit de corps*, to give my executives the leeway to develop their imagination, adaptability, and versatility, to foresee the unforeseeable, to control overhead expenses, to invent with an eye to the inevitable uncertainties of the future."

Bernt went to the fireplace, lit the paper and the firewood with his lighter. The flame flew upward, deepening the shadows, enveloping the logs. An aroma of pine filled the room.

"We cannot do without fire; even in summer we light one on the terrace of our estate on the island of Storö. There we grill the fish we catch in the archipelago."

"Do you have a boat?"

"Yes. The children have learned to handle the sails, dive like porpoises, pick the wild orchids on the islets, gather berries and mushrooms, watch for the flight of the migratory birds."

He described Viveca, his tall, brunette daughter, and Lars and Axel, his two blond sons. There were no photographs of them in the room. Bernt asked Pierre if he were married.

"No."

"We men haven't changed since the days when we

departed to hunt reindeer or bison. We left our wives and children hidden away deep in the heart of a cavern. What really excites us is adventure, competing, testing ourselves to the utmost. When grandfather named me to succeed him as president of the Group, I accepted the appointment as a challenge. One might say that my success was a foregone conclusion. I knew how my uncle and cousins felt about me. They were too afraid of the head of the clan to dispute his decision. Very early, when I was young, he had formed me in his image. They have never forgiven me."

Bernt emptied his glass and immediately refilled it. The embers of the fire, the alcohol, and the wind whistling through the branches made Pierre feel torpid, dreamy. He imagined himself sitting at this table, a pile of paper next to him. He would have written so hard and so long that he would have forgotten to eat. In such heavenly solitude, enclosed by the murmurings of the forest, by the lakes, the torrents, the rivers, he would have come to an understanding of his own heart, laid bare at last.

"Another sandwich? Some cheese?" Bernt asked.

Pierre refused. Thirteen hundred kilometers to the north of Stockholm, it was strange to be sharing a common solitude, to have come upon such a close fellowship, which was all the more powerful for being a gift free of any ties. In two hours they would part forever. Bernt stared at the sparks flying from the dry wood. His nose, which curved downward from his forehead, his thick, arched eyebrows, his eyes set aslant, formed a physical harmony of which he seemed unaware. He was preoccupied by a single thought.

"Why were you chosen instead of your father?" Pierre inquired.

Bernt threw two logs on the fire, then leaned back, his drink in his hand.

"Grandfather thought that I was more qualified, I suppose. He lived only for the business that he had created. He came from a family of farmers. In the winter they were lumberjacks, cutting down and transporting pines, oaks, and birches. Trees occupy over half the surface of Sweden, where the arable land doesn't reach over nine percent, so they have become almost pantheistic objects for us. Grandfather was more ambitious than the rest of his family, and obtained a scholarship. He had grasped the fact that only the highest level of education would permit him to change class and rise in the social hierarchy. He became a specialist in economics and foresaw the strides that could be made in wood by-products. He married a girl he had met at the university, who possessed the advantage of being the daughter of a wealthy banker, and went into business for himself. With such assets in his favor, he devoted himself completely to becoming a successful business tycoon. He controlled banks and paper mills, held majority control over electricity and compressed-air machinery factories, and so on. When I was five years old, he told me that I was to be his heir and that I must prove myself capable of fulfilling the responsibilities that he would hand over to me one day. My father and his brother Carl were victims, in a sense. One was trained in Germany and the other in England to enable them to expand the power of the Group, but they were not up to the ambitions of its chief. I probably succeeded because there was a span of two gen-

erations between us. His desire for power left no
breathing space for interlocutors, business allies, or
family. Fully aware of his superior mental faculties,
his discernment, and his practical ability, he did not
hesitate to make quick decisions, he refused to permit
his projects to be interfered with or even to accept
advice. He held himself to be above the laws govern-
ing other mortals. When he fell in love, which occurred at least a dozen times, he did not hide his
affairs. He generally chose his beautiful and delightful mistresses from among the fashionable social
classes. He was not satisfied with having married its
finest flower; he had to possess new buds constantly.
A veritable hothouse of roses! When Grandmother
dared reproach him for his infidelities—though she
knew that it was hopeless to try and change his behavior one iota—he merely reminded her that she had
married the whole man and that she must take the
good with the bad. My father suffered from this dis-
play of vitality. Of a retiring, introverted nature, like
his brother Carl, he couldn't hide his irritation when
Grandfather, who preferred the monologue to the dialogue, exposed his theories at the dinner table while
eating an enormous meal. After having drunk his
coffee, he would shut himself up in his office, even on
weekends. He made no secret of the fact that his
family bored him. He could stay up until all hours of
the night without tiring, right up to the age of eighty.
He refused to cede his place to anyone, let alone to
his two sons, whom he detested because they would
be alive when death's jaws had finally seized him. His
favorite sport was to humiliate them. He pretended to
ask their advice, and then, after they had given it, he
would draw up a contrary plan whose subtlety would

reveal to what degree Nils and Carl were lacking in imagination and enterprise. He did this to prove to them that, despite the handicap of being thirty years their senior, he was still the great Lars. He regarded his children as rivals and made it a point of honor that they should not outstrip him. As a result, Nils, my father, did not dare to take any initiative and Carl, my uncle, developed a talent for dissimulation equal to his rancor against humanity."

"Didn't your grandmother try to protect her sons?"

Bernt tasted a slice of smoked herring.

"She respected her husband too highly and was very much in love with him. Only Grandfather's ideas, which he received from heaven and carried out the moment they were conceived, were of any importance. His talent for rapid action served the old pirate well. He traveled constantly. His poverty-stricken youth led him to save money for a rainy day; he had a particular flair for foreseeing what combination of circumstances might arise in a given situation. He bought low, sold almost always at the peak. Only a week after his mother's death, he was making important deals in Wall Street. No sorrow could ever prevent him from pocketing a profit. The Americans who met him in New York that week were surprised to learn that he had just returned from his mother's funeral; no one could have imagined such a thing because of the reverent attention he gave to his investments.

"He was always able to lay his hands on the capital needed to take over the majority in a business that he coveted. He composed a list of companies whose control seemed to him indispensable to the equilibrium of his investment complex; as soon as he bought one, he would cross its name off the piece of paper that he always kept on his person. The paper had begun to turn yellow with age when he crossed out the last one, but his plan had been executed. He turned to me proudly and said: 'You see, my son, no one has ever succeeded in holding out against me!'

"And that was true—except for my mother. He would never have dreamed that his son Nils, who was interested mainly in botany—the worst possible defect in Lars's eyes—would be capable of bringing home a girl in whose eyes there was a gleam that he recognized, for it was like his own. At seventeen, Lena was made of the same metal as the most powerful man in Sweden, who was fifty-six. He was struck by her resemblance to himself. Daughter of an impractical dreamer, an architect, a scrupulous esthete, she came from Dalecarlia, the most beautiful of the Swedish provinces. Father and daughter went off to watch for the passage of the wild ducks and the polar swans, studied the Elizabethan tragedies together, searched for mushrooms, listened at night to Mozart, Bach, and Grieg in their secluded house, isolated by the icy winter that gives rise to phantoms and arcane dreams. My mother, from whom emanated a mysterious aura, was in communication with the invisible forces of nature.

"Grandfather was responsive to her charm, but he also feared it. Since he was not a man to beat about the bush, he tried to stop the marriage, finding it inadmissible that such an exceptional creature should belong to the 'botanist.' He invented obstacles which did not survive the least examination, took refuge in caprices, declaring that he refused to give his consent to such an absurd union.

"My father, who was twenty-five at the time, had always bowed before the authority of the head of the family, but the passion he felt for his fiancée had transformed him. He declared that he would leave Sweden for England with her and that he was determined to marry her in the face of all opposition. Lars understood that if his obstinacy persisted he would only cause a rupture. He pretended to give in to pressure from his wife, who could not understand his position. In Sweden, a difference in social standing or affluence plays little part. Each person has his chance at the start; the class concept has become blurred, money is less important than personal merit. Lena's beauty and intelligence were such that only in bad faith could one refuse such an irreproachable girl, whose father enjoyed a fine reputation. Lars's position against the marriage was regarded as a momentary whim, and the wedding took place in Dalecarlia in the month of June. However, Grandfather's opposition had succeeded in causing a rift between father and son. Nils was convinced that his father had opposed the marriage out of gratuitous spite, and furthermore considered it a flagrant insult against his wife.

"The following summer, Lars broke with the two mistresses whom he had been keeping, in order to devote himself to his family. He installed stables on his estate on the island of Storö that were as fine as those of the king. He took jumping lessons and went for long rides in the forest with his daughter-in-law. Lena, my mother, was a remarkable horsewoman and delighted to have her own horse. She discovered that the formidable head of the clan was an attentive man who took her opinions seriously, and even solicited them. My grandfather soon decided that Nils should travel for the Group. He put him in charge of the international division, making him responsible for foreign trade. In those days people traveled by sea, which meant that Nils was away a great deal of the time. Lena was bored in his absence, and soon Lars, who had noted her fine intelligence, proposed that she work for him.

"My mother was blessed with perfect health, a taste for taking risks, and a sense of initiative. As Lars's personal assistant, she became so fascinated by her work that she never missed a meeting, including one held the day before she gave birth to me. What would her life have been if she had not drowned during a fishing trip, when I was almost two? My grandfather's despair knew no bounds. He built her a tomb at Storö; he insisted that the sculptor represent her leaning on an elbow, her eyes wide open, like those recumbent Etruscan figures awaiting the moment of resurrection. He worked eighteen hours a day, wearing out his staff, trying unsuccessfully to forget the lovely girl from Dalecarlia.

"My father left the business. Traumatized by the loss of his wife, he retired to the Norwegian frontier to manage a forest of two thousand hectares that he had inherited from his mother. Luther said that man must accomplish his own salvation. Nils created for himself a religion of remorse, of doubt; he examined and reexamined his life. Though he did not go to church, he felt the need to believe; anxiety was eating him up. There was, alas, no cure, because an inner block prevented him from recognizing a dissimulated obsession that he concealed even from himself.

"He had left it to old Lars to see to my education. From the start my grandfather exercised tremendous pressure on me to insure that I would become the instrument that would carry his ambitions to their zenith. Besides the Scandinavian languages, I learned Russian, German, English, and French. I was rarely permitted any distractions or amusements. If I asked to take flying lessons, my request's fulfillment or denial depended upon an abstract program that had been decided upon once and for all. Whether it involved a hamster, an orange, a voyage, a girl I had been forbidden to see—all was dependent upon the imperatives of my future as head of a dynasty. I had been warned that sacrifices would be demanded of me and I fulfilled them, aware of the good fortune, the lofty destiny that awaited me.

"We aren't easy on young boys. They must learn to stand punishment, to be *tuffa*, like those figureheads sculpted by the Vikings on the bows of ships to confront the ocean waves. As a schoolboy, I spent vacations as an apprentice woodsman in Lapland. I know how to saw down a tree, leaving the stump as smooth as a baby's cheek. I fished for cod three months aboard a schooner, I sold newspapers and tourist guides in the street to earn pocket money, but I was forbidden to buy a motorcycle, to listen to jazz records, or to go dancing in a discothèque. My lot was different from that of my schoolmates, for whom it was considered normal to have a girl friend at the age of fifteen. I did not feel as though I belonged to a group representing the most independent and most privileged youth in Europe. I had traded my freedom in against the promise of a future that would be clothed in power and authority when I reached adulthood, and the exchange seemed to me perfectly equitable.

"On my eighteenth birthday, Grandfather called me into his immense office in his bank. I loved that room with its mahogany-paneled walls and comfortable leather sofa and armchairs. A map of the world occupied one panel of a wall. It was mounted on a magnetic plaque, which allowed him to move the arrows and the multicolored metal buttons that illustrated his strategy, when he was speaking with his associates. He sat me down on the couch facing him and announced his final decision to make me his heir. He was counting on me to expand the key industries of our Group, particularly in the research sector.

"After my graduation from the Harvard Business School, Grandfather installed me in an office next to his. It was luxuriously decorated, since he knew very well that people usually take the external signs of power for power itself. He initiated me into the arcane mysteries of his affairs, taught me to read the financial journals, and imparted to me his secret method of judging others accurately. That man, who owned eleven percent of the companies in Sweden and whose associates as well as his rivals trembled in awe before him, treated me with a delicacy and a tact such as I have never come across in another human being. He transferred to me the affection and interest he had felt for my mother. At an age when he felt that he had nothing more to expect from love, I was the miracle, his alter ego. He appreciated the asceticism which I had imposed upon myself in order to pass my examinations with honors.

"I worked by his side, my eyes fixed on the balance sheets. Our walls were covered with graphs, proudly portraying the ascending lines that indicated our constantly increasing profits. At the age of twenty-five, I suddenly began to feel the need for new sensations, fresh experiences. In short, I was seized with a rage to live. I had enough of being the means by which my grandfather intended to prolong his reign, of merely being his intermediary—in fact his prisoner. I negotiated as an equal with the Fords, the Agnellis, the Rothschilds, the Rockefellers, whose Monets, Renoirs, Braques, and Picassos were similar to those hanging in our home in Stockholm. Their signed furniture, their rare porcelain, their stamped silver did not differ one iota from ours. In contrast to the Vikings, who pushed their excursions as far as Asia, the only god I respected was Grandfather, whose influence equalled that of a chief of state—his word was a treaty, his signature an edict. His iron hand lay heavy on my shoulder. The days of my youth were rigorous; they slipped away in accordance with a timetable that led me to spend sixteen hours a day working under the control of an autocrat who was intolerant of the least frivolity, such as idling away time in a bookstore, traveling for pleasure, spending an evening with the girl of my choice. He was worried about my susceptibility to passion, because he feared that I might marry someone of whom he didn't approve. The Minotaur with whom I had signed a pact demanded that I sacrifice not only my freedom but also my emotions."

Bernt had finished his beer. The logs were burned to embers. He threw some wood on the fire, then went to the kitchen and returned with another bottle, which he poured carefully to avoid the foam.

"Despite my desire to escape, I couldn't change. We're too well known here. When I telephoned to a client, even abroad, my family name was immediately recognized; I suffered from living in a glass house, condemned to be regarded as a sort of robot. Since I didn't have the right to be myself, I devoted myself to the god of duty. Despite my uncle Carl's intrigues, Grandfather gave me room for more and more initiative. I learned to manage our affairs during international crises, to evaluate the sectors that were slowing down, to plan where our efforts should be concentrated. There were no signs that could point out the dangers to us in time to avoid them; we had to prepare in advance before the market showed signs of weakness, so that we could adjust to unpredictable turns of events. And there Grandfather's flair was incomparable. In addition to wood industries, we were involved in turbines, generators, electric machinery, parts for oil tankers, all of which implied a certain familiarity with the men in power. A minimum of invitations to dinner are necessary to gain influence. I maintained friendly relations with our cabinet ministers, and thus was informed of governmental decisions before they were revealed to the newspapers, which permitted us to get an idea of the lay of the land. This game of anticipating what might occur absorbed me completely. Against such odds, a woman could not count for much. Mothers followed my movements closely, but I was careful not to compromise their daughters in any way. We didn't speak the same language. Their frivolous world, the restricted circle in which they moved, the sentimental problems that they exaggerated in order to give themselves the illusion of being alive, their preoccupation with fashion, horse racing, children, recipes, bored me to death. When I traveled abroad, however, the women became exotic plumed birds that I caressed and tamed.

They tried to keep me with them, those fresh-faced Americans, Italian princesses, Australian beauties, but to no avail. After some delightful conversation, a dance, and a night in each other's arms, I would blow a kiss and fly away, forging ahead to more important things. I helped them to forget me rather quickly by never replying to their love letters. When I had drunk my fill of foreign pleasures, recklessly shaking off my yoke, their silhouettes disappeared as quickly as the desire that had seized me.

"Once the plane had taken off from Stockholm, I began to float in a cloud of fantasies; I was a seagull, a migratory bird, flying over forests and oceans. I knew that I was gifted enough to persuade an adversary to come to an agreement, to win an impossible business deal, to sign an inconceivably good contract. I landed in New York, Amsterdam, Frankfurt, or Sydney prepared to do eager battle with my peers, whom I sometimes met in a private room reserved for us at the airport. After the battle was won, or deferred, we would relax and enjoy each other's company in the best restaurant in town. I would usually end up in the arms of the lady I had chosen for the evening.

"In Stockholm, I was protected from the temptations to pleasure offered me elsewhere. At home, I concentrated on such problems as how to insure that the Group could weather the storms we were facing, how we could expand our commercial activities in a period of large-scale industrial development and hold our place in the modern world by making critical changes and transformations. My blood was stirred by the challenge, and I plunged into my work like a bathyscaphe diving three thousand meters to the bottom of the sea, my mind icily lucid.

"'You are stronger than I; you have no heart,' remarked my grandfather, who came to the office every day but no longer made any decisions without first consulting me.

"At the close of business, we remained alone in the skyscraper of glass and steel that he had built in the ultramodern business section. The view of the city was sensational, the lights seeming to beckon us to a night of dissipation and pleasure. The telephone was silent. We had no need to explain ourselves—our mutual understanding was biological. Besides, we had told each other almost everything. He had described his various love affairs and had asked me pertinent questions about my own life, paying closer attention to me than a mother. My seduction technique rarely varied: a look exchanged, consent obtained, bed, a romantic breakfast, then the eternal plane once again. Grandfather looked thoughtful.

"'My boy, you are almost twenty-six and I am eighty-five.'

"I gazed at his wrinkled face, his pale blue eyes, his thick mane of white hair. He stood straight as a ramrod and had succeeded in keeping the slim figure of his youth by riding horseback and swimming every day. I began to reassure him about his physical strength, but he interrupted me:

"'I will be happy only when I know that your son will be at my bedside when I die. It is time to think of that, Bernt.'

"I suddenly felt resentful. Grandfather had warned me against Italy: 'Take care. The climate is bad for us. Tuscany can make us lose our head—and I have need of yours.'

"The preceding year, I had been to Milan to conclude a business deal. Suddenly I felt the need to escape from such an industrial city into the lovely light of Umbria, Assisi, Gubbio. I roamed the alleyways of Florence among those palaces whose golden stone still vibrates with the passions of the Renaissance, and whose statues are lit from within by a secret life. I was in Siena the day of the Palio festival, my head spinning as I watched people dressed in doublets and bicolored breeches, looking as if they had stepped out of a museum painting. Half the city opposed the other half. The most peaceful people were transformed into Gorgons if their side showed signs of losing. I was transported four centuries into the past by the race with its caparisoned horses, its scarlet oriflammes, its multicolored banners. I had forgotten the papers accumulating on my desk in Stockholm and was feverishly absorbed by the spectacle. Ah!—the roll of the drums of the curly-headed young men wearing red berets, the checkered reins of a gentleman whose green cape matched his horse's blanket, the parade of Renaissance men against the ocher background of churches and palaces, the cries, the cheers, the roars of laughter! Next to me in the stands stood an Italian woman, a golden chain circling her blond hair. She shouted when the Blues won, clapping her hands with delight. A Swedish woman would never have shown such passionate enthusiasm. She was ravishingly beautiful.

"It was a simple matter to engage her in conversation, to invite her to dinner in a *trattoria*, to accompany her at midnight to her home and to wake up in her arms the next morning. Donatella, married to an agricultural engineer busy irrigating the southern tip of the peninsula, revealed to me that I might be capa-

ble of relaxing my vigilant hold on the helm of our
business. Telegrams were sent to me in Siena, but
never reached me. Grandfather confided to me later
that he had been so upset by my escapade that he
had thought of choosing another successor. In Siena, I
was content to love a woman who did not belong to
me. When I entered her body, I had the impression
that I was possessing a land polished by art, refinement, desire, where everything is civilized and
good taste abounds along with passion. I had become
one of those cavaliers incapable of paying attention to
anything other than love. Donatella had taken the
place of the Group's charts and my devotion to duty.
She sang me a verse of Lorenzo de' Medici's:

> How beautiful is the springtime of life!
> But, weary, the youthful years flee.
> Let all joy be tasted today.
> Of the coming day, there is naught to reassure us.

"The visage of my cold severe city of twenty-four
islands had disappeared, had given way to balconies
covered with flowers, to songs rising from the street,
to summer and warmth, my memories scattered by
the ever-renewed embraces of a woman who possessed me completely.

"One morning her husband telephoned to say that
he was returning. She accompanied me to the airport.
I can still taste her tears on my lips.

"And here was Grandfather speaking to me of marriage! I was obliged to yield. I knew him well enough
to be certain that he had not left his choice to chance,
but had consulted the *Taxeringskalender*."

"The *Taxeringskalender*?" asked Pierre.

Bernt jumped as though he had forgotten Pierre's presence. The wind howled outside the pavilion, the trees bent by its force, as though in pain.

"It's the bedside reading of the bourgeoisie. The parents leaf through this almanach as soon as their child begins to flirt seriously, so as to check up on the social and financial background of the other's family. It is similar to the principal evening paper that publishes the photographs of the richest taxpayers, giving the sum in the caption. Grandfather held a high position on that list, and my wife, as a matter of course, was bound to come from a similar social and financial background. Old Lars was essentially feudal.

"He placed his homes in Stockholm and on the island of Storö at my disposal so that I could give a series of receptions to which a proper selection of young ladies would be invited. I was engaged by the following spring.

"Ingrid was twenty years old, had beautiful clear skin and the body of a fine swimmer. What reason could I have given for refusing to marry her? Her father was involved in the food and chemical industries; she was a blue-chip investment. She admired me; she was sweet and sincere; she was sure to give me a healthy heir. Lars was born three months before his grandfather died in a fall from his horse. At least I am certain that *he* was pleased with me. This was not the case with my wife.

"Ingrid found it difficult to accept the fact that I often came home from the office at ten in the evening. It was imperative that I remain in contact with New York, Melbourne, Tokyo, so I had established a rotating work schedule with my secretaries to insure that I always had one at my disposal twelve hours a day.

But Ingrid had no inner resources, and depended upon me for diversion. Her friends' husbands came home at five in the afternoon, and she couldn't understand why I should be different. She bored me, and I was irritated to see that the mother of my children had an exceedingly banal mind. She gradually came to acquire a degree of independence and no longer demanded of me what I was incapable of giving her. She knew that she would always receive a jewel for her birthday, that I would spend two weeks during the summer with her and the children at Storö. Though my hours displeased her, at least I came home every night. Twice a month we gave dinner parties, bringing together the most prominent people in the country—industrialists, financiers, cabinet ministers. Ingrid received her guests with the same cold elegance that she displayed in bed. She behaved like a decorous, deferential partner, showing neither anger nor indignation now that she had accepted my way of life as inevitable. A far cry indeed from Donatella!

"I bowed to her wishes regarding the education of our three children. She believed in one of my grandfather's favorite principles—perfection in all things. Our children were handsome, their manners perfect, their grades acceptable. I was fond of them, but I never had much to say to them. Our most intimate moments together were spent fishing for salmon or sailing our boat.

"I was never tempted to be unfaithful to Ingrid. The wives of our friends were interchangeable with her—the same black dress made by the best dress designer in Stockholm, the same pearls, the same books, and identical interests."

Bernt fell silent. The empty beer bottles lay on the tray like ninepins. Pierre inquired:

"How old are you? Thirty-nine?"

"Why do you ask?"

Pierre spoke slowly.

"You are at the head of an industrial empire. Your desires can always be fulfilled. If you should wish to buy a house in Japan, it would belong to you the very next day. If you should want to spend a week in Siberia to experience at first hand what Solzhenitsyn describes in his books, your secretary can make the necessary reservations. You are free to fly away to Nepal, even to talk with the masters of China, should you wish to sell one of your products to them. You can buy a Rembrandt, start a collection of rare objects or modern paintings. There is no obstacle barring your way. And nevertheless, you are tormented by doubt and anguish. Novelists are curious insects with sensitive antennae. You asked me to accompany you because you suspected that you could trust me."

Bernt scrutinized him in silence, then replied:

"I have nothing to lose. You would certainly have done better to sleep in Kiruna. It is undoubtedly the hope that I may give you some ideas for one of your future books that keeps you awake."

He stood up, took several steps towards the window, drew aside the velvet drape, and leaned his forehead against the pane of glass, as though the whirls of snowflakes had the power to chase away his torment.

IV

THOUGH THE INTENSITY OF FEELING THAT STEMMED from being in the presence of one of his fictitious *personnages* was extremely exhausting, Pierre's mental faculties were sharpened by the fact that his surroundings were so unfamiliar. He tried to guess what secret ghosts were hidden behind Bernt's story. He felt responsible for him, wanted to comfort him, to help him find peace during the too few hours left them to converse together. At the same time, Bernt had given Pierre the courage to match his own convictions with his actions, to see things clearly without hiding from the consequences. He had come to realize just how little Leonore meant to him. He determined to break with her upon his return to Paris, rather than remain a victim of habit, fearful of what the future might hold.

Pierre could not explain the bond of intimacy that

had been forged between himself and Bernt. Although the financial domain was unfamiliar to him, he understood Bernt's thoughts as though they were his own. He generally felt aloof from others, somehow different. He could not remember when it had been otherwise. His schoolmates had complained bitterly when their mothers inspected their socks for holes, or wrote to them demanding immediate replies, or searched for pornographic novels hidden under their pillows, or read their private letters and diaries, or came to see the principal regularly to check up on their studies. They had envied him Vera's beauty, her gaiety, her liberal spirit, her youth, not understanding how much indifference was hidden behind the façade. She was interested in only one person—herself—and such narcissism excluded her son. He accepted this as a fact of life against which it would be useless to revolt, believing that it was his own fault, that he was not worthy of keeping her attention focused on him or of arousing her tenderness. He felt awkward in society, embarrassed by his body, clumsy in sports. He took refuge in his imagination, projecting personal fantasies which could never disappoint him. When he wrote down his dreams, the miracle was accomplished.

Pierre had suffered from a mother's neglect; Bernt had never known his. Pierre's father had been killed in 1943; Bernt's father had abandoned him by retiring to a château near the Norwegian frontier. They had both been raised by their grandparents. They had both suffered at a young age from a lack of tenderness, and their wounds had remained deep because of that lack.

Pierre realized how little he knew about economics

as he listened to his companion describe the origin of
a disagreement he had had with his uncle Carl and
his cousins regarding the construction of a naval base.
The words "investments," "balance sheets," and "price
advantages" held slight meaning for him. He lived
like a perpetual student. His articles and his broad-
casts permitted him to get along fairly well, but he
had no sense of collective responsibility. On the other
hand, at a very young age, Bernt had become responsible for a pyramid of companies, and this had ma-
tured him. Was that what lay at the origin of his
difficulties? How could he be taught to relax and enjoy himself? His rigorous upbringing seemed to have
prevented the Swede from tackling those questions
which were most important to him. He was blocked
from truly confiding in anyone; and Pierre was not
the man to force the issue.

Bernt asked him to come and see his bedroom.

The staircase was carpeted in emerald green.
Several doors opened off the landing, the walls of
which were covered with the stuffed heads of rein-
deers, does, wolves baring powerful fangs. The handsome furniture with its decorative inlaid patterns, the
beautiful carved lamps, and the Chinese porcelain
were surprising to find in this house lost in the middle
of a forest. They entered Bernt's room, which was
carpeted in turquoise. Paintings by Nicolas de Stael,
romantic and tortured despite their clarity of vision,
were hanging on the beige walls; a table formed from
a block of crystal and cube-shaped armchairs bore the
signature of a famous modern designer. Bernt threw
himself down on the fur coverlet spread over his bed.
He pointed to the desk piled high with business
documents.

"Whenever I have a delicate problem to cope with, I try to resolve it here. This place is conducive to reflection. I don't possess the genius of my grandfather, who was primitive enough to be guided by his instincts."

Reclining in an armchair, his legs stretched out on a huge square footstool, Pierre listened attentively. This was the first time that a character shaped in his imagination had taken human form. He never began to write a novel without knowing thoroughly beforehand the political opinions, the profession, the tastes, the religious beliefs, the physique, the ancestors, the childhood of the being he proposed to describe at a selected crucial point in his existence. He might ruminate about the character for one or two years. When he finally saw the person clearly, he would free him or her to roam the landscape that was most suitable. The rest came easily, requiring only concentrated work.

Was he interested in Bernt merely out of professional curiosity? Perhaps he was inspecting him as the coleopter hunter examines the butterfly caught in his net.

Bernt's references to his grandfather, who had died several years earlier, betrayed to what extent he had been marked by the authoritarian old man. He tried to explain this away by claiming that it was normal to feel grateful to the man to whom he owed everything. Bernt's voice rose, became emphatic. He threw his jacket and tie onto a white leather chair, crossed his arms behind his head, and blew smoke rings towards the ceiling. The branches rattling in the wind's blasts, the rustle of the budding leaves, lulled them as though they were aboard a phantom vessel sailing on a sea in the black of night.

"All that happened so long ago," said Bernt. "No one has had so austere a youth as mine. For a long time I took ambition to mean only the search for authority or even superiority; I couldn't conceive of any pleasure equal to that of acquiring power and responsibilities. The intelligence of the master who was guiding me, his wealth of experience, and his absence of scruples were of inestimable value to me. But at his death, the difficulties began. His will confirmed, wihout equivocation, my appointment as his successor, and stated that his son Carl and my cousins were to assist me. Though my grandfather's personality was sufficiently contradictory to evoke controversy, nobody would ever have accused him of naïveté. He had believed that his authority was so well established that his choice would be respected automatically. He sinned by an excess of confidence in himself; he had underestimated his second son. Although my father had retired, Uncle Carl continued his participation as an associate in the Group. Grandfather couldn't bear him. After one particularly stormy executive meeting, he beckoned me to follow him to his office, where he strode up and down like a tiger in a cage. 'Have you ever seen such an impossible creature? Why does he try to oppose me in such an underhanded fashion? Hypocrite! I put him in his place. Watch him, Bernt. He will try to cause you trouble, I know it!'

"His eyes blazed with anger under his thick, bushy eyebrows; but there was also a gleam of affectionate irony, which was revealed only to me. I felt that the others judged him far too unjustly. Perhaps he felt a certain tenderness towards me because I was the only one to stand up to him. There was no great merit in that, since I was free as a bird. I had few material needs. A pair of velours trousers, a sweater, a fishing skiff, these sufficed to make me content. I was able to remain silent for days, as was my grandfather. We were aware of our weaknesses and our capabilities. He faced death without anxiety because he knew that I would succeed him. Once he had gone, my uncle Carl began his attempt to undermine me. He found it intolerable to be serving on a board of directors presided over by his nephew. The pain of bereavement is usually tempered by the bequests the parent leaves behind; but Carl's position was not altered by his father's death. He was still director of our company in charge of the factory making prefabricated houses, but it was I who had inherited the estate on the island of Storö, the sumptuous private house in Stockholm, Grandfather's collections of impressionist paintings and rare Chinese porcelain.

"I had believed that the obstacles I was bound to face would arise from my own character. The extent of my vulnerability had been revealed to me by the love I had encountered in Italy. The haunting, obsessive memory of an old love is comparable to those illnesses which are accompanied by mysterious remissions and relapses. When it suddenly assailed me, Donatella's image would obliterate the years; I only ceased to suffer by immersing myself in work. There is no problem that cannot be effaced by a day of furious activity. With the passing of the years, I became Ingrid's model husband, working incessantly, relaxing only on Sunday to sail with the children around the tiny islands of the archipalego, where the gulls would fly in ever-higher circles over our heads. I held myself firmly in check, avoiding trips to Italy or to France. Love implies perfect truth and understanding. It is free of all those servitudes stemming from our lack of courage and of faith. It is pure contemplation, eager to dispense with whatever falls short of its expectations. I had lost the key to a forgotten language—and that was all to the good.

"Money itself did not seem to me any more debasing than a field of corn that I might have inherited instead. I was asked to take care of it, choose the seeds, sow them and reap the profits. My work more than satisfied me. When my secretary brought me the morning mail, I was impatient to discover what battles were to be faced, what prey was about to fall into the nets I had spread. I had projects to plan, long-term stalking schemes to prepare. Those reflections kept me in a euphoric state until the daily meeting with my associates. I took care to give them enough confidence to dare express themselves openly, without fear, presenting objections to me as well as suggestions. I preferred true counselors to flatterers who do not really merit their salary. This meant that I had at my disposal a string of aides whose work made it possible for me to concentrate on my more important activities. We formed a single bloc, though there were some who an excess of zeal sometimes incited to compete with their colleagues. I reminded them that in the best interests of the Group we must conserve our energy for the battles with those on the outside and refrain from wasting it on internecine quarrels—which happens all too often in most large companies. The family that I had created with those ardent, active young men who believed in me, and who would have worked by my side until midnight if I so requested, became closer to me than Ingrid and my children, who could not share my interests and who have constantly complained that they saw too little of me.

"Lars, my eldest son, resembles my father. At eleven, he is timid and introverted and finds it difficult to express himself. As to the younger children, Viveca is nine and Axel seven, too young to really interest me. I always preferred the company of my staff aides, whose enthusiasm intoxicated me with the same thrill as the Vikings must have felt when they loaded food and arms on their ships to set sail for unknown lands. Although Sweden has not suffered from invasions since the sixteenth century, nor participated in world conflicts, those meetings in which we formed our battle plans metamorphosed us into a virile group of men similar to the military in wartime. I was the leader of a battalion of fanatics, capable of mounting an assault on reputedly impregnable fortresses. My second in command, Otto, to whom I had given power of attorney, understood my thoughts even before I had finished formulating them, and at our meetings he gave discourses rich in ideas and projects. Although there is only seven years difference in age between us, I would like to have had a son who resembled him."

An owl beat its wings and hooted. Bernt put out his cigarette in a quartz ashtray and lit another before lying down again. He spoke softly, as though to himself:

"Carl never understood that I was putting at everyone's disposal the invaluable experience acquired during my time spent with a financial genius. He accused me of overweening ambition, not realizing that I have always had few personal needs. Instead of my grandfather's château I would have been content with a bungalow. A fishing smack would have served me just as well as our yacht with its crew of four. I kept the house in Stockholm and its park out of superstition rather than respect for tradition. We Swedes have a predilection for the imaginary, the supernatural, an aptitude for perceiving the invisible. That residence seemed beneficent. The great Lars had acquired it when he married, and he had furnished it with care; it had witnessed the crowning of his success. I intended to pass it on to my eldest son."

Bernt leaned on an elbow, brushing an ash from his flannel trousers.

"Carl was allergic to the idea of seeing us installed in my father's house, just as he couldn't bear to see me occupying the presidential office. The wound caused by Grandfather's choice of me as his heir healed badly. The least shock reopened it. He could never look me straight in the eye. Of slight build, balding, he has always walked with a slight limp due to a defect in his hip. He does not at all resemble Lars, who had inherited the athletic constitution of the woodsmen of the North. Did Carl resent the fact that I resembled his father more than he did? Our intercourse was based on necessity. He found it difficult to hide his aversion to me, although the secondary position that he occupied in the firm had accustomed him to dissimulate his feelings. He lay in wait for years while setting a trap for his prey. Yet his children drew checks on our banks; a paper company belonging to the Group hired his son-in-law. Under my direction, there was an augmentation of nine percent in our profits. What did he have to complain about?"

Ten days ago, Bernt had been studying a confidential document when his secretary informed him that someone who did not have an appointment wished to see him about an urgent personal matter. Otto was instructed to see the person instead. He came to Bernt's office several minutes later to say that the visitor, a woman, had refused to talk with him, insisting that her message was for the president's ears only. Bernt sighed and pushed aside his papers. Experience had taught him that people should never be sent away before they revealed what had brought them in the first place. Everything seemed to be working at cross-purposes that day. Ingrid had gotten it into her head to rent a villa in the south of France for the summer. She was bored with the idea of Storö, with vacations where nothing new ever happened, with a large house difficult to take care of, in which so many rooms lay useless and empty. Bernt had informed her that he would not change his program. As he left for the office, she proffered threats, which was singularly unlike her, declaring that she would fly alone to Nice with the children, that he was too egotistical, et cetera. At the office, he learned that Christer Linders, shipowner and head of the shipbuilding firm into which he wanted to buy, had canceled the meeting to confirm the understanding that they had been pursuing for two months. Pressure had obviously been brought to bear upon Linders, causing him to step back from an agreement he had been ready to sign. Nothing was ever completed; the businesses run by the Group were made up of tirelessly rewoven cloth. The initial strategy used with regard to the shipowner would have to be reconsidered; enormous patience was required.

Otto stood stiffly before him, his manner deferential, his eyes alive with interest. Bernt opened his drawer to put away the papers on which he had been taking notes.

"Who is it?"

"Here's her card."

Ulla Uwersen. The name evoked no recognition. The address was that of a new section of ultramodern apartment buildings, to the west of the town.

"Tell her to come in." He decided to give her ten minutes of his time to get the matter over with.

She entered the room, slim and graceful in a suit of black wool. He could not remember ever having seen such narrow hips, nor such extraordinary jade-colored eyes fringed with coal-black lashes. Her brown hair was pulled back into a low knot on the nape of her neck. Her face was unusual; her slanting green eyes stared at him with such intensity that he was forced to turn his head slightly away from such brilliance. He was moved by her low, hoarse, sensual voice.

"I'm Christer Linders's daughter, and I have come to inform you about certain facts of which you may be unaware."

She was seated facing him, not far from Lars's enormous map of the world, whose curve was accentuated by a ray of winter sun. Her legs, crossed at the knee, were beautifully curved; her feet, small for a Swedish girl, were shod with lovely shoes that fit like gloves. Bernt was usually able to concentrate completely on his interlocutor so that he could immediately capture any hidden nuances. Once he had determined to which psychological category the person belonged, he had only to adopt the approach that seemed appropriate to the case. But this time his system was not working. This woman distracted his attention. He tried to take himself in hand, and coldly asked what had brought her to see him.

She explained that she had introduced herself by her husband's name so as to be certain that Bernt would receive her, since she assumed that he might be angry with her shipowner father. She was in a position, she asserted, to reveal the problem that lay behind the affair. Bernt did not wish to admit to this self-assured young woman that he was ignorant of the problem to which she referred. All he knew was that Christer Linders had been on the verge of signing an agreement with the Group, but had broken the appointment, putting it off to a later, undesignated date.

"Why did your father cancel our meeting? He should have been sitting in that armchair in your place."

She gave him a keen glance. He was still under the spell of her beauty, and he realized that she knew how to use it to the best advantage. He imagined such force let loose in his arms, in bed, and pulled his thoughts together to erase the image, staring at the framed graphs, their lines rising proudly as proof of the Group's constant increase in holdings and profits. She explained that Carl had come to see the shipowner, recommending the utmost discretion. He had warned her father that a reorganization was soon to take place and that as a result he, Carl, would become president and Bernt would be out of power. He had also declared that, although he had not yet closely examined the ship-construction documents, he was, of course, aware that large investments were in-

volved. He promised to study them with a favorable
eye at a later date. In the meantime, he suggested, it
would be preferable if the shipowner were to abstain
from confirming a contract which, in view of the circumstances, might become null and void.

She continued: "My father had met your uncle
many times, since they belong to the same club. He
had no reason to doubt his word, and therefore he
thought it more sensible to wait. He is still prepared
to sign with you, if you can assure him that you will
continue on as president of the Group."

The storm had subsided. Bernt was once again
coldly lucid, fully aware of the danger he was facing.

"Who sent you here?"

"I came on my own. I've been working with my father since I came of age. I studied the terms and conditions you proposed for our association with you,
and I approved wholeheartedly!"

Ulla Uwersen smiled, looking very young and ap-
pealing as she did so.

"You are well known, you are respected, you have
the reputation of being supremely efficient. I don't see
why we shouldn't sign this agreement."

She had suggested to her father that she make this
visit to clear up the matter. If Carl heard of it, he
would put it down to the initiative of an impulsive
young woman. She had felt the need to see Bernt in
order to get to the bottom of the affair, to be sure of
all the relevant facts.

So, ruminated Bernt, Carl had been the instigator
of maneuvers aimed at impeding the smooth running
of the Group! He had taken up once again the battle
that he had tried to wage when the old pirate had
been alive. If Bernt wished to conserve his freedom of

action, he must rely upon a consensus within the direction of the Group that would dispense him from being obliged to justify his ventures. His uncle would never forgive him for the affection showered upon him by the founder of the dynasty, for their intimacy, for the position he had given Bernt at his side, for the presidency of the Group that Bernt had inherited. Because of Carl's allotment of shares, uncle and nephew were condemned to work together. The former coveted his nephew's position of power rather than his financial standing. Neither of them held a majority of the stock; the arbitrator was Nils, who had remarried and was living on his property at the northern frontier with Norway, occupying himself with the exploitation of his forest. Bernt wondered whether he should visit him. He could not overcome a feeling of constraint with the father who had gone away and left him. They shared no memories that might have made it possible to create some kind of intimate communication. Bernt made an effort to be agreeable when they met, but their conversations were always difficult to sustain. He found his stepmother mediocre and dull, though he appreciated the fact that she was a fine housekeeper and seemed to make her husband relatively happy.

Ulla continued:

"Neither our associates nor our clients approve of family squabbles. We must be assured that you will remain in a position of power and will be capable of frustrating the plots that are being prepared against you."

How young she was, Bernt reflected. But her youthful enthusiasm would one day bend before the setbacks she was bound to meet; she would begin to doubt herself, until finally she would give in to routine and carefully obey all the accepted rules—unless, of course, she should become a past mistress at using her obvious talents to their best advantage. Comparing himself to her, Bernt judged to what degree his forty years had marked him, penetrated his defences, without his having been aware of it. Accustomed as he was to the schemes formulated in the quiet dining rooms of private clubs, whose results appeared several weeks later—public offers to buy, spectacular rises or falls in the stock market, company presidents brought low, forced to surrender before being pushed out of the businesses that had been their life's work, triumphant newcomers reveling in the newfound victory; inured as he had become to hard knocks, his skin marked with still-sensitive scars, he nevertheless continued to be astonished at the fact that others could hate him, though he had never sought to harm anyone. A rare and therefore dangerous fury invaded him as he contemplated the image of his uncle Carl slipping away to see one of the most powerful men in Stockholm, Christer Linders, in order to plant a rumor, spitting venom aimed at the moral assassination of his nephew and at undermining negotiations which Bernt had brought to the point of fruition.

"Are you absolutely certain of the truth of what you are telling me?" he asked.

She replied in a cool, incisive voice:

"Your uncle has undoubtedly not boasted of his visit. We thought his approach tasteless, although he tried to justify it by claiming that he wished to save us from making a mistake. I repeat that he asked us to keep his visit secret."

"Then why have you broken your promise?"

Ulla sparkled with vitality. It was surprising that he had never met her at one or another reception. He would have noticed her immediately. Since she was fifteen years younger than he, she probably frequented other social circles. It was touching to see her take her work so seriously, throw herself into it so completely, attempt to minimize her beauty by dressing severely, adopt the language of businessmen.

"Your agreement appeals to us. It would help us to expand certain projects, particularly those concerning the drilling in the North Sea. We were ready to sign with you, but your uncle's visit has prompted us to be prudent. We are compelled to wait until any doubt is dispelled. When the difficulties between you two are solved, I shall convince my father to take up negotiations with you once again."

"Why are you being so helpful?"

Her green eyes revealed a flicker of amusement.

"We are aware of your dynamism, your personal reputation, the confidence your organization enjoys. It would not be the same if your uncle, whose character leaves something to be desired, were the president."

"I won't forget what you have done, Madame Uwersen."

The understatement of her clothes, her quiet elegance, did not succeed in concealing the veiled and sensual radiance of her beauty, which played upon his nerves and his senses. He felt a cold and savage excitement in his belly. He had an overwhelming desire to take her in his arms, to tear off her clothes and possess her then and there. He closed his eyes for a second, pulled himself together and collected his thoughts.

"There is nothing ambiguous about my position. I shall remain as president of the Group. Christer Linders has only to ask his legal advisors to see mine, and he will be reassured on that score."

He was becoming extremely nervous, and tried as best he could to control himself.

"May I contact you within a few days, or should I get in touch with your father instead?"

"You may telephone me directly," she replied.

Bernt accompanied her to the elevator, surprised to catch himself quivering in anticipation of another meeting.

V

Bernt liked to be the last to leave the office. He enjoyed the solitude, free at last of the office routines, the interminable conversations, the insistent telephone calls, that collective existence whose pace had, however, become indispensable to him. Bernt felt most alive when he was busiest, assailed by successive visitors requesting his opinion about complicated questions, constantly being interrupted by telephone calls from New York or San Francisco. His agreement, his verdict, his final word were awaited with impatience so that a deal might be concluded. His decision was binding and resulted in the investment of capital, the hiring or transferring of personnel, the creation of new jobs and new factories, the suppression of another company. He arranged mergers between his rivals and the Group, would buy a business, then resell it three years later at a considerable profit. When he decided to part with a company, he thought only of the figures on the balance sheet, never of the reactions of the staff, sold like cattle to other directors who might perhaps fire them immediately. How could he get to know the hundred thousand people who were dependent upon him? If the laws of good business practice dictated severance from a company and handing it over to another corporation, Bernt could see only the possible profit involved. His decisions to dispense with one company or to buy another were purely abstract and had no relation to the human factor involved. The personal dramas that sometimes resulted rarely reached his level, but were handled by his executive staff. He was shielded from the reach of the outside world; he associated only with pleasant, courteous people who wished to please him, or aides like Otto who would gladly have sacrificed themselves for him. He was the leader of an army who pitted himself against other sovereigns, his adversaries, openly on the battlefield, his helmet off, his mask tossed aside. Bernt entered into combat with full knowledge of what he was about, and his jousts ended in either spectacular ruin or grandiose conquest. He was in the habit of ruling, of being surrounded by deferent, intelligent men who would suggest ideas but then bow happily to his decision. Carl's treason was thus an exceedingly bitter pill to swallow. Bernt was seized by a helpless rage. His unyielding resolution, the concentration of his willpower, were an expression of his inner determination to pursue a specific course rather than a desire to affirm his superiority by triumphing over exterior obstacles. He sighed. Who would have imagined that his uncle—that funny little man who fluttered about like an insect, compensating for his physical shortcomings by wearing handsomely cut tweeds made to order for him by the best tailor in London—was obsessed with working out plans to bring about his nephew's downfall? Of course it is impossible to foresee the absurd. Bernt tried to recall earlier board meetings, staff conferences, brief personal dialogues. When President Nasser of Egypt was about to receive a new foreign chief of state, he would spread on his desk about twenty photographs of the person and examine them closely to uncover the one revelatory detail that would deliver the key to the man with whom he would be dealing. Bernt tried to call to mind the expressions of Carl's face, with its shifty eyes, a face that was excessively self-controlled, with rarely, a spontaneous movement or sign of an impulse of solidarity. Carl's reflexes had become corroded by a jealousy born of fear. For years he had been concealing his envy, a dark tide that had captured his mind and heart. It would have been useless to attempt to win him over, to make peace with him. His nephew was his eternal enemy. How could Bernt ward off the storm that was brewing?

There was a knock at the door. The tall, slightly stooped figure of Otto entered the room. Otto was eminently qualified to succeed him, but the family would never agree to that. Installed in the office immediately next to Bernt's, Otto worked on his papers far past the hour when most of the other senior staff members had left, and he was always at his superior's disposition. Bernt's refuge was his office, with its large bay window, the graphs, the map of the world, the shelves crowded with leather-bound books, his grandfather's armchair, rather than his home, where Ingrid tried to maintain a semblance of intimacy and where he felt cold and lonely, attempting to avoid the penetrating looks she gave him.

"Do you want us to examine the Jorgensen affair together, sir?"

"No, Otto. I'm going home now. I have something to take care of there."

Bernt's respect for the clan won out over his need to share his anxiety. Despite his confidence in Otto, in his tact, in his faculties of perception and judgment, he did not dare destroy the myth of the royal family. An impassable barrier lay between the members of the dynasty and those in their professional entourage. It was better that he not tell Otto of Carl's disloyalty. He could not bring himself to speak of the conversation with Ulla. Once again Bernt had to shoulder alone the responsibility for a major decision.

He stood up, put his hand on Otto's shoulder, picked up his red leather briefcase, and waved goodbye. His chauffeur was waiting for him in the black limousine in which he would sign his correspondence, study a report, or read the evening newspapers.

He did not converse with Werner, the chauffeur, but instead ruminated about Carl's hatred, which concealed itself under the cover of familial affection. Was his uncle jealous of what he considered to be Bernt's excessive good fortune? Had he forgotten that Bernt had been unlucky in losing his mother at such a young age that he had no memory of her? Whenever the wind moaned and the wood crackled in the fireplace, he imagined that Lena's poor lost soul was trying to communicate with him, her hair streaming in the green water, her eyes open to the sky, continuing to toss and turn in the waves which served as her shroud! Nils had not been able to save her. He had been rescued, haggard, hysterical, incapable of furnishing any explanation for the accident. For the rest of his life, Bernt was to miss that maternal tenderness. Siena had given him a glimpse of it, and many a time his nostalgia for those days with Donatella invaded his heart.

Red stop signs blocked the Mercedes. The city seemed so well organized that it was hard to imagine that it left any room for fantasy. But Bernt knew its potential for folly and extravagant acts. In December, when the Nobel Prize was awarded and Stockholm was lit up like a Christmas tree, dancers ran through the streets, drunk with joy in the night lit by stars and candle flames. From time to time the icy conventions melted, liberating an effervescence of passion. Was it so bad after all to live in a country where the politicians were honest, the law incorruptible, personal freedom respected, social conflicts abolished? Women enjoyed the same rights as men, prostitution had practically been abolished except in elegant clubs where, after the erotic spectacle which had taken place in public, one could retire to a small room for a price, either to photograph a nude girl or to demand special sexual treatment. Bernt had never done so. He was too concerned about his respectability to indulge in such practices. The high regard for quality, which tended to reduce class differences, was accompanied by the idea of continuous self-improvement. There were study sessions, cultural associations, whose purpose was to teach a second trade, a new craft or art, higher specialized skills. In these sessions, the camaraderie and physical warmth evoked broke the circle of anguish and shadows by giving the illusion that people were communicating intimately with one another from a firm basis of shared faith which pushed back the frontiers of solitude. Pastry shops and tearooms took the place of French cafés; meetings were even held there. Before dispersing and venturing out into the snow to return home, people would discuss the ideas that had just been assimilated and then set another rendezvous.

Bernt remembered well those nights of *Valborgsmassoafton*, when he was a student and celebrated the coming of spring on the thirtieth of April. The ice cracked under the pressure of the living forces underneath, the flowers burst into bloom, the leaves appeared on the trees, the birds warbled to announce the coming of summer, the season for love. It was the reverse of that long night, when everything became tinged with profound melancholy, inspiring an unutterable nostalgia for light. Then, the human soul became invaded by the same sadness and the same primitive fear that had seized human beings in the first years of humanity's existence, a sadness and a fear based on the obscurity of our beginnings, the maternal mystery. Ignorant of notions of space and time, men had feared that daylight would remain forever buried, that the solar barque would remain anchored in that invisible, corresponding domain, the refuge of the dead, and that the moon would reign supreme. They prayed in their clumsy tongue for the return of the star that was depriving them of light in order to punish them for their sins. On the eve of the first of May, springtime brought pardon and deliverance. It was a gala occasion, as they rejoiced in divine protection. Today, the students belonging to different clubs insult each other, challenge each other, while farmers and sailors celebrate with akvavit the end of the fearful night, and villagers and townsmen dance and sing together.

The car crossed over two bridges. The reflections of the neon lights showed up for the space of an instant the expressions of the passersby. Were they frightened by the spectre of an overly predictable future? Any apprentice earned more than a skilled worker elsewhere in Europe. He knew what to expect: marriage; several rooms in which his wife, tired out from a day of housework, would shout at the children, who preferred to play rather than to do their homework; alcohol, which would help him to endure those around him when night seemed endless. Happily, there would be the days when he would hasten to live to the fullest, to strike a fish in a torrent, to gather wild flowers or mushrooms under an ever-changing sky whose mysterious light accords a respite to men's pains.

The chauffeur entered an avenue planted with trees and bordered with estates, where homes were hidden within well-cared-for parks. What did Ingrid have to complain about? Although servants were almost impossible to come by, she had a Yugoslav couple who took care of the cleaning, cooking, and serving. She had only to telephone to give an order and it would be delivered within the hour. The silver gleamed, there was not a spot of dust anywhere, no task required her presence. She enjoyed fixing the vases, filling them with lovely flowers and leaves from the garden, and arranging them with some talent, for which she deserved to be complimented.

The car stopped before the park's entrance gate. Ljubo ran to open it. A cedar of Lebanon stood straight and stark, its branches congealed by frost; a clump of beeches was buried in snow. Bernt greeted the valet, then strode up the freshly raked walk. He crossed the lawn, entered the hallway. Flemish tapestries covered the walls behind the marble tables. A stone staircase ornamented with a wrought-iron banister went up to a gallery on the second floor where Dutch still lifes were hung. Old Lars had done things very well indeed. In a way, Carl's rancor was understandable. Each room contained one or several works by Renoir, Monet, Sisley, Vlaminck, Cezanne, Dunoyer de Segonzac. Only the paintings of Picasso, which his grandfather had not appreciated, were lacking.

Ingrid had furnished for herself a small salon whose windows looked out on the garden. She liked to stay there during the day rather than use one of the large reception rooms on the ground floor.

She was talking with one of her friends, the wife of the president of the court of appeals. Dina announced the opening of a club for those young people who had just finished a detoxification cure. They needed to readapt themselves to normal life, and the club would serve as good neutral ground. She asked Ingrid if she would consent to work there as a volunteer.

In twelve years of marriage, Ingrid had slid from the stage of being a young girl to the threshold of maturity. Her blond hair pulled severely back and held in place by a velvet ribbon, the creases at the corners of her eyes, and her respectable air already conjured up the woman of forty-five that she would become in ten years or so. An aroma of soap emanated from her, mundane remarks filled her conversation, she was a diligent hostess. He was probably responsible for her lack of self-assurance, her lack of radiance. She bored him. Was she aware of it? She had given him three handsome children who had never caused them any trouble; she was extremely elegant, and usually even-tempered. What did he have to reproach her for?—except that she stirred up no enthusiasm in him, no passion, no divine madness.

Bernt pulled up a chair to sit near the women on the sofa. He asked Dina questions about the club, politely feigning an interest he did not feel. Ingrid asked him if she should accept Dina's proposal.

"Do as you please. What difference can it possibly make to me if you take care of those poor kids or spend your time playing bridge!" he replied.

The magistrate's wife threw him a reproachful look. He changed the subject. Why didn't she leave? He became increasingly irritated, although he knew that he was being unjust. Dina described the bombing of Dresden, which she had witnessed. At dawn, she had slipped out of the cellar where she had spent the night. The buildings, the churches, the museum, the station, the city hall, the houses had all been leveled to the ground, leaving only a field of burnt, stony, black rubble. She described the absolute silence, the mysterious horror of the martyred city. This woman who had lived through such war experiences still carried her scars. Bernt was grateful to his country for having remained neutral. Dina got up.

"I must hurry! George hates to find the house empty when he turns the key in the lock. It's enough to put him in a bad humor until the next morning. Telephone me, darling. We'll see how many hours you might be able to give us."

When Dina's car had turned the corner of the

driveway, Ingrid rejoined Bernt with a decorous smile. Was she telling herself that it was time to play her role as the mistress of the house who is greeting her husband at the end of a day's work? He followed her into the salon where, on the piano, an immense floral bouquet was arranged. She pushed a button, which lit up the impressionist paintings. Bernt was captivated by Monet's garden of poppies under a rosy gray sky. In his mind's eye he entered the park enclosed by an ivory-colored wall, accompanied with slow steps down a sandy lane the smiling young woman in a straw hat secured by a veil knotted under her chin. She resembled the kind of women with whom he had a tendency to fall in love—a subtle charm mingled with a great deal of natural ease of manner.

"Would you like something to drink, Bernt?"

He repressed a gesture of impatience. When on earth was Ingrid going to be herself? They were like two guests facing one another. He had nothing to reproach her for except that she left his mind at rest, empty of thought and emotion. She was beautiful, however, with regular features, pretty blue eyes, a youthful air, a harmonious silhouette. She came to his side and poured some whisky into a crystal goblet. Bernt swallowed it at one draught and was surprised at the consolation it brought him.

"How is it that you are home so early today?" Ingrid asked.

He knew that he could count on her discretion, and so he told her of Ulla Uwersen's visit.

"What would you do if you were me?" he inquired.

"You're asking *me* that?"

He disliked her humility. He was not unaware that

he was difficult to live with and that he belonged to a privileged caste. The newspapers talked of his family, printed his photograph; the international economic reviews had listed him among the most powerful corporation heads in the world. Was that any reason for his wife to be so timid? His relations with her were ambiguous. They shared no secret code, no smiles or jokes to which they alone held the key. She was incapable of the least initiative, inhibited by the personality of her husband.

"I can visit Carl to try to sound him out, but he will surely lie, hide his true feelings and attitudes, slip through my fingers like a fish. Aside from his sons, who holds enough shares to swing a majority? My father! I can't believe that he would come to an understanding with his brother against me without first discussing it with me."

"Anything is possible," Ingrid replied.

"I must go to see him. I'm his son, after all. He'll tell me the truth!"

Nils's behavior was strange. No one knew what he had suffered when he had given up his rights. He had never expressed a regret. His new company, the management of his forests, seemed to absorb him completely. He showed almost total indifference toward his grandchildren, who barely knew him. He refused to visit them during the summer at Storö, perhaps because of the tragic memory of the accident that had occurred there.

Ingrid walked to the back of Bernt's chair and leaned her elbows on his shoulders. Her cheek brushed against his thick hair. The odor of dried herbs and tobacco rose from her husband. She leaned more heavily against him.

A door slammed; the sound of footsteps echoed from the marble floors. She smiled.

"The children are back from the swimming pool."

They invaded the salon, all talking at the same time, boasting of the speed records they had broken in the hundred-meter race. Why worry? His children represented the sole reply to the future. Bernt thrust aside his misgivings to involve himself with their concerns. It was perhaps just as well that he grant himself twelve hours respite.

VI

How was it possible for a person to live in such a remote place for forty years? After Lena's funeral, Nils had informed his father that he no longer wanted to remain with the Group. Not even taking the time to say good-bye to Bernt, who was living with his grandparents, he had moved immediately to his stone fortress on the Norwegian frontier. Lars never revealed what he and his son had said to each other. Pale, and so impressively calm that his associates had not dared ask for an explanation or hazard a comment, old Lars had informed them that his eldest son had decided to resign in order to manage a property that he had inherited. Since the right to personal privacy is inviolable in Sweden, it was considered indiscreet even to think of questioning the fact that Nils had chosen to exploit a forest rather than to rise in the world of business.

Bernt had rented a car at the airport to drive the fifty kilometers to his father's house, set in a curve of rocky mountains, a refuge for birds of prey, incessantly battered by howling winds. He knew that the meeting would be difficult. Determined to bury himself in total solitude, Nils had limited his visits to Stockholm to several days once or twice a year, and had never bothered to hide his indifference toward his son, to whom, moreover, he never wrote. Bernt recalled his father's sudden appearances at Christmas, when he would give him a toy and absentmindedly inquire how he was doing in school, filling them both with an acute desire to end such a useless dialogue as quickly as possible. Bernt had become inured to the absence of such an inadequate father. Formal politeness cannot serve as a substitute for a life led together, cannot replace the sharing of common memories of intimate, sometimes tender moments of joy and sorrow, delight and anger.

During his adolescence, Bernt had yearned for his father's presence so that he might ask for guidance. When he became interested in girls, books could not teach him how to attract them, how to vanquish the timidity that paralyzed him; if his father had been at his side, Bernt could have confided in him. Then too, together they might have stood up to that authoritarian pressure of the head of the clan, whereas alone Bernt had no recourse against his grandfather's domination.

His father's silence over the years had wounded Bernt deeply and had left many unhealed scars. At bottom he suffered from a vague feeling of guilt, from an obscure idea that perhaps Nils had chosen to keep aloof because his son did not come up to his expecta-

tions, had disappointed him. Worst of all for Bernt
was his inability to put his finger on what offense he
had committed. There were times when he thought
that perhaps he was being punished for simply exist-
ing.

He had been sent to the best schools in Stockholm
by his grandparents, who were responsible for his
education. Lars's gruff affection finally cured him of
his obsession with the paternal myth. When his marriage to Ingrid had been decided, Bernt had made
this same journey in order to introduce his fiancée to
Nils. Father and son had been ill-at-ease with each
other from start to finish. Bernt had found it impossible to break through his father's icy exterior. Nils had
remarried. His wife was a brunette twenty-five years
his junior. He had informed the family of his new
marriage after it had taken place, without explaining
how they had met. Bernt was convinced that his father
had met his wife in a bar one evening when he had
drunk enough akvavit to blunt his judgment, and that
she had been experienced enough with men to know
how to handle him. Amazed and delighted at having
succeeded in getting Nils to marry her, she had con-
sented to live with him in his remote retreat. She was
probably still delighted to be sleeping in a soft, can-
opied bed and counting the piles of linen heaped up
in her Norwegian closets.

Nils was content making his rounds, checking those
giant trees which were to be chopped down. He loved
the odor of sawdust, the muffled sound of the blows
of woodcutters' axes, the sharp explosions of electric
saws, and the shouts of the men as they pushed the
carts loaded with fallen trees to the river banks.
Sometimes a woodsman would attach a small plastic

box to a tree trunk, containing a message destined for a worker at the port where the wood was eventually to end up after its voyage down the river.

Bernt really knew very little about his strange father. He doubted that Nils had agreed with Carl to the dismissal of his own son without any warning. Given Nils's character, it seemed unlikely, but Bernt had learned to beware of making snap judgments about human nature, for it could take many strange turns. He was prepared for a possible nasty shock.

There were no houses or villages along the road bordered by interminable rows of fir trees. What did Bernt hope to accomplish by this impulsive visit? Ulla Uwersen had telephoned him two days earlier to ask if he had cleared up the situation with his uncle, since her father was impatiently waiting to sign a contract with the Group. Bernt had immediately decided to take a plane to consult with his father.

He took a crossroad winding up the side of the mountain. Huge rocks crushed the ivy that carpeted the ground to the feet of the fir trees. Hidden behind a thick layer of clouds, the sun was beginning to set and the leaden sky was turning black. Bernt accelerated. When they had spoken on the telephone, Nils had asked him to stay for dinner, but Bernt had reserved a seat back to Stockholm on the plane leaving that same evening. If the affair were settled by the end of the afternoon, he saw no reason to stay the night.

He entered a paved, somber courtyard bordered with yew trees. In the large entrance hall filled with hunting trophies, Nils greeted him with reserve, without any outward show of affection, bowed slightly and asked if he had had a pleasant trip.

Confronting this pale, chilly man with expressionless eyes, so obviously in command of himself, Bernt wondered how to approach the matter, how to bring about a mutual exchange of views, how to strike a spark of understanding. When meeting for the first time with a man about whom he knew very little and with whom he was intending to set up a complex business affair, he would first try to detect his hidden nature, to discover his hidden motivations, by engaging in a conversation that would reveal his opponent's attitudes toward foreign policy, economic problems, the prime minister, etc. After two or three replies, Bernt would know with whom he was dealing and how he should handle him. But he was at a loss before a father who might as well have been encased in armor as impenetrable as that worn by the knights in the Middle Ages. Nils's life in his retreat at the edge of a ravine covered with fir trees bore no relation to that of a businessman; the twenty-eight years that lay between them might have been a century.

Bernt followed him into the paneled drawing room, where a tree trunk was burning in the fireplace. The fire threw an orange glow over the stone tiles and the thick wool rugs. A table of black wood ran along the front of the bookshelves, which were overflowing with scientific works. With one gulp, Bernt drank the akvavit offered by his father.

"Where is your wife?"

"I thought that since you were taking the trouble to come to see me of your own volition, which you have never done before, you must surely have something on your mind that you would prefer to discuss with me privately."

His father's polite smile, the slight inclination of his

head, reminded Bernt of nothing so much as a Japanese ritual. How was he to convince this man not to abandon his son a second time? He sat down in a comfortable armchair and watched the strange patterns the flames made at the bottom of his glass.

"I assume that Ingrid and the children are well," his father continued. "But then that isn't what really interests you, is it? You live only for the Group. My father succeeded in inoculating you with his virus. I was able to escape in time. I study astronomy and biology; I subscribe to medical journals from all over the world. This kind of existence enriches me far more than your headlong race for money."

Bernt protested that he was not involved in a race for money at all. He declared that he felt himself responsible for a living organism that must be expanded and developed, and that he never failed to face challenges that demanded he advance as far as possible, even beyond his immediate objectives.

Nils seemed to wither before his eyes. He passed a hand over his forehead as though to efface a shadow.

"You speak exactly like my father. I recognize his phraseology. He thought only of himself, loved only himself. He considered his business triumphs to be an homage to his own genius, and he used them to celebrate the cult of himself."

Although Nils spoke softly, it was evident that the years had not erased his anger.

"What do you suppose that I came here to find? I had no choice; it was my only chance for survival! He would have destroyed me! I refused to believe in him unconditionally, to be his disciple, and he refused to accept less from those close to him. You weren't able to escape. When he took you in hand, he was at the

height of his reign; how could a child resist his influence? He permitted no arbitrator or any intervention
other than his own. He was the opposite of a liberal
spirit. Flatterers found him easy prey; it sufficed to
praise him, to frequent his mistresses. Don't you agree
with me, Bernt? If you only knew!"

Nils resembled a scholar because of his eagle-beak
nose, his crown of gray hair, his reserved manner, and
the wool turtleneck sweater he wore under his tweed
jacket to protect him from the drafts of air that circu-
lated throughout the house. Under his reserve there
ran a flood of repressed passion. Bernt had always
wondered why his father had left him. Now for the
first time they were completely alone. The occasion
would perhaps not present itself again. He decided to
take the risk of asking the question that he had
mulled over so often.

"Why did you hand me over to your parents rather
than take me with you?"

Nils got up to tend the fire. He leaned down
towards the burning embers, his back to Bernt.

"Must you really know the reason?"

Bernt suddenly felt uneasy, as though a hot iron
were entering his soul. He was unused to being so hy-
persensitive, certain as he was of his impeccable
business judgment and secure in his stable family life.
He wished that he had not asked the question, but it
was too late.

Nils sat down in a chair studded with silver nails.
His face was wooden, the vertical lines from nostrils
to chin accentuating his monkish aspect; he could
have served as a model for Dürer. He appeared to
hesitate as he stared at his son. The only sound in the
room was the ticking of the clock.

"It's painful for me to talk about a difficult situation that I have finally surmounted. If you have the courage, if you consider that you are adult enough, strong enough to hear it, I will tell you about it. Give me your word that you will say nothing of this to your wife or to your children. The secrets of the dead belong to them alone."

Bernt felt trapped. He would have been happy to see his father's wife appear, so that the conversation might change. Nils was watching him carefully from under half-closed lids. Bernt said nothing, awaiting an explanation. His father took his silence for assent.

"I met your mother at the university in Stockholm. At seventeen, she resembled a lovely swan. Her father, a rather original type, had brought her up in close contact with nature, whose signs she had learned to interpret. She understood the language of animals and the cries of the migratory birds, discerned the anxiety that seized them at the end of summer, when they develop an irresistible compulsion to fly south. In September, the fog transformed her surroundings into a gray mass in which contours and reliefs disappeared. Though unable to see them, she heard the cries of thousands of wild ducks which, according to her nurse whom she believed implicitly, took refuge in the moon during the long winter months.

"Lena's charm overwhelmed me. I was timid; my father had almost emasculated me. He was always on the lookout for a revelation of my shortcomings, his manner ironic as though to prove that he had been right in treating me as an imbecile. How did I convince that beautiful fellow student to go out with me and then agree to become my wife? By a passion so violent that she could not resist. I couldn't believe my luck. I had discovered an exceptional being who, by God knows what miracle, had agreed to be mine. Her confidence in me cured me of my inhibitions. My father had closed my horizon, had kept me from profiting from my youth. My mother had given way completely to her husband's caprices. We lived in constant terror of his anger, his rejection, his changing moods. We were forced to clench our fists and keep a stiff upper lip as we submitted to his will. I'm ashamed to confess that even when I was twenty-two he still frightened me. I was repelled by my cowardice, by my uneasiness when he spoke to me. His sharp, curt voice demolished me. I often dreamt of his death. I imagined that the ship he had just boarded en route to the United States would founder on a rock, saw his car running smack into a wall, his broken body no longer dangerous. I would then have taken over his role beside my mother and become the head of the Group. At other times, I would picture him in exile, having divorced my mother and left us to marry a French woman and live in Paris. Lena rescued me from such fantasies by restoring to me the pleasures of the sea and the mountains. When I looked into her eyes, I was able to accept myself as I was. Mama insisted on receiving Lena alone one afternoon. She too feared my father, although she loved him. She wanted to have a prior conversation with Lena in order to be better able to act as a buffer between my father and myself in case of a scene. Touched by Lena's delicacy and beauty, Mama congratulated me and asked that I bring her to the house the following week. She promised that she would be solidly on our side if there were any trouble with my father.

"That Sunday in June, 1932, Lena wore a chiffon dress with a rose at her belt. I picked her up at the lodging house where she lived. Mama had placed the garden chairs under the beech trees, around a table loaded with fruit juices, goblets, biscuits, and cake. Carl and my cousins fell silent when we appeared. Minutes later Lena was a full-fledged member of the assemblage, and Mama was smiling benignly.

"My father, who was working in his library, did not appear until teatime. Normally, once he had finished his second cup, he would return to his papers and no one would have dared interrupt him. I was delighted to see Lena so relaxed and tranquil with my family. When he arrived, handsome and imperious, he went to greet her first. She looked at him calmly as he questioned her closely about her studies, her family. My old timidity overcame me, and I didn't have the courage to take part in their conversation. Slowly, I perceived that Lena had no need of my help. She made my father laugh several times, inquired about his business and his projects—quite naturally, as though she were a person a hostess had placed next to him at dinner with the admonition to charm him. He remained with us until evening, and suggested to Lena that she stay to dinner. She refused, to my relief, since I wanted so much to be alone with her. The following week, Papa asked me to come to Storö, and suggested that I bring Lena if I thought that would please her. The visit was a nightmare for me. He took her sailing, dragged her off to see the Viking tombs, invented an automobile excursion that excluded the rest of the family. Lena, with great tact, calmed me, telling me that I should be glad that he was nice to her, that he was not dangerous, given his age, that in any case she loved me.

"I was therefore completely astonished when, in the autumn, Mama informed me that Papa had decided against our marriage, declaring that as his eldest son and heir I could make a better match. His unjust attitude made me furious. Now that I had passed my final exams in political science and economics, I was able to get up enough courage to declare that I preferred to break with the family rather than obey such a stupid decision. Mama played intermediary; I fixed the date for our marriage; Father finally gave in.

"During our honeymoon, I reveled in my sweet revenge. I was delighted to have carried off such a victory over a person who had terrified me for so many years. My marriage seemed to me the summit of love, since it enabled me to give my name to my beloved, to be free to give her a child, to know that she was mine completely and that innumerable years stretched before us in which we could live out our love in the closest possible intimacy.

"On our return, my father did not bother us. He seemed to have accepted our marriage. Whenever I made disagreeable remarks about him, Lena would defend him. She was impressed with his power, his genius, his success; she didn't recognize his monstrous side, his devilish nature. Probably he had succeeded in captivating her with his life story, which he embellished considerably for her benefit. I was working very hard. The Group had just been reorganized and I had been put in charge of the foreign department.

"It was cruel to impose so many trips abroad on a young bridegroom. If I had not been the son of the president and founder, I would have protested, but my position gave me less freedom than if I had been an ordinary member of the staff. I was so afraid of being accused of profiting from my family relationship in order to benefit from unjustified privileges that I allowed myself to be badly treated. Lena offered to speak to my father, but I dissuaded her from doing so. He was so vindictive that he would have made me pay in one way or another for what he would have considered to be a lack of responsibility. I couldn't count on him to make my career easier; he was tougher on me than on the others. It was best not to give him a pretext to exercise his severity. I persuaded Lena that the business trips wouldn't last for long. Soon, I told her, I would have earned my freedom and would return to Stockholm in a stronger position.

"Letters from my wife accumulated in the hotels of America and the Orient. Lena's news surprised me: My father had offered her a position in the business. She had accepted because she could not endure being idle. When I returned to Sweden, I discovered that she spoke the jargon of businessmen and was completely dedicated to her job. I tried to smother her newfound knowledge with my kisses, but she pushed me away. I refused to listen to her; she punished me by refusing to be docile. What did I have to tell her? Without her by my side, I had lost the desire to visit the Taj Mahal or Bangkok. I restricted myself to visiting our clients and, when I was not getting drunk in my hotel bar, wrote to her during the long, lonely evenings. I was heartsick for her, filled with anger, as I wondered how I could escape from such a web. When I spoke of my feelings to Lena during my re-

turns to Stockholm (at that time we traveled by sea
and I was absent for months on end), she pretended
not to understand. She began to change; slowly she
moved away from me, and I could do nothing about
it. When we were alone, she hurriedly inquired about
my business abroad, about the local customs—so as to
avoid more dangerous subjects. She invited friends,
kept us busy going out to dinner parties, and generally insured that we led an active social life. Our relationship had become so false, so artificial, that we
could barely hide our relief at being forced to separate once again. Who was responsible for that fiasco,
since we loved each other so much? My passion for
Lena turned to despair. At night she would usually
try to elude my embraces, or else accepted my lovemaking with such passivity that I felt she was counting the stars in the design on the ceiling.

"No one could help me. Alone during those ship
crossings, I had time to think over our situation. I
loved Lena. The estrangement she felt was due to our
long separations. Deprived of our intimacy over the
months, how could we possibly evolve in the same
direction? I was grateful to my father for having introduced her into the business world, thus giving her
energy and her intelligence an outlet, but at the same
time he had liberated in her forces that I could not
succeed in mastering. He had supplied her with an
office and a secretary. She was young. At that time
women rarely were given such responsibility, and she
couldn't avoid having her head turned. When I was
home, which occurred rarely, she opened the evening
paper to the financial page. Had I been older, it
would have made me smile; I would have understood
that she was heady with a kind of power that had

made many another lose his judgment. Many of my father's dinner guests were civil servants, or businessmen who had become government ministers by a chance cabinet shuffle. They came to consider it normal that they have at their disposal a car and chauffeur as well as expensive furniture that did not belong to them, normal to be recognized on sight by passersby in the street. It wouldn't have taken much for them to speak of themselves in the third person. Numerous pretty women were taken in by the myth these people incarnated. They caused a great deal of trouble between husbands and wives, sometimes breaking up marriages. When a new turn of the merry-go-round sent them back to 'civilian' life, they lapsed into nervous depressions, their court was dissolved, the pretty ladies who had desired them were now busy charming their successors. They even had to buy their own railway tickets. Their demoralization ceased only with the hope of a new spin along the enchanted byways of power.

"At the other end of the world, I found it difficult to concentrate on selling our products to Japanese industrialists. As I tossed and turned in my bed, unable to sleep, I decided that there was only one possible solution—I would have to stop traveling and stay with my wife if my marriage were to succeed.

"On my return to Stockholm, I asked my father for an appointment, which he put off for several days. It was impossible to discuss anything with him during our family dinners. I noticed the deference with which he treated my wife. He forgot the difference in their ages. He leaned toward her to solicit her opinion, to offer his own ideas. He had lost his sense of reality. That man, one of the most exceptional in Sweden, deposited his power at her feet.

"My mother appeared calm, her serenity unshaken. I had tea with her as I had in my youth. I loved that rite in the English tradition, the table covered with a damask cloth and set out with porcelain and silver, toast, butter, cake, jam, and marmalade. When we were children, such a tea was regarded as our reward for good behavior. My mother's hair had whitened, her eyesight was beginning to fail, but she still held herself like a queen and presided over the table with the same elegance as in my childhood. I explained to her that my father's influence over Lena in my absence had so estranged her from me that I had decided to stop my business travels abroad. Mother sighed as she held out the sugar to me, and said that everything would depend on my father's wishes.

"I shouted that I was capable of leaving the family and taking a job elsewhere, even with a competitor, that I loved Lena and that she was more important to me than the establishment of markets in the Orient. My mother tried to calm me, which increased my fury.

" 'Why do you refuse to help me? Are you that afraid of your husband? Are you his slave? Or are you trying to break up my marriage because you're jealous of Lena?'

"She lost her self-possession and replied: 'Do you think it's easy? What can I do? He can't do without her anymore. You know what he's like! He's interested only in his own pleasure; he disregards the consequences of his actions. He believes that his genius puts him above the law. I've tried to reason with him,

to make clear to him that he was doing her harm—
and you. But he refused to listen.'

"Mama explained to me that Lars had become so
enraptured with his daughter-in-law that Lena exercised an excessively strong hold over him. At that
point, I began to worry that Lena might not approve
of my idea of returning to Stockholm for good.

"Mama went on: 'At sixty a man is more formidable
than at twenty-five, because he has prestige, taste,
savoir-faire.'

"She was opening new horizons for me. Was Lars
trying to seduce Lena? The number of years separating them rendered this hypothesis absurd, ridiculous,
impossible! I asked Mama if she meant that Lena had
been flirting with Papa. She replied that she was sure
such was not the case, but she felt their intimacy to
be exceedingly unhealthy.

"That conversation shook me and sowed poisoned
seeds in my mind. That same evening, I made imper-
tinent remarks about my father to Lena. She defended him passionately. I then realized that the
situation was far more dangerous than I had believed.
She identified with him wholly, he had won her over
completely.

" 'He's a remarkable man, an admirable man! If you
only knew how patient he's been with me, what he's
taught me! He's a man who deserves one's total confidence. You're too hard on him; you attack him because of your pride, though you would be nothing if
it weren't for him!'

"I was wild with rage. Finally, exhausted and exasperated, we ended up sleeping apart—Lena in our
bedroom, I in the living room. She must have spoken
about this to my father, because the very next day he

granted me the appointment that a week earlier I had requested.

"He was waiting for me, standing next to his desk, his hand on the globe of the world. He asked what the trouble was.

"Lars was in the habit of putting his adversary on the defensive. He had forgotten that I was his son. I didn't bother to reply, but simply sat down in one of the armchairs, obliging him to sit next to me, thus depriving him of the advantage of being protected by his desk.

"He repeated: 'What's the problem, Nils?'

"I replied that I had no problem, that I was blessed with a wonderful wife whom I loved and a profession that interested me, that I was perfectly happy. He seemed disconcerted, and asked why, in that case, I had wanted this meeting with him.

"I crossed my legs and slowly lit a cigarette. I was in no hurry. His position was more delicate than mine.

" 'For personal reasons, I wish to cease my activities in America and in the Orient. After two years of constant travel, I want to give it up.'

"He tried to suppress his anger. His blue eyes had turned almost black. 'Ah, and what do you propose to do?'

" 'You have a staff of thousands. Give me another job.'

"He launched into a tirade about the discipline required of heirs to a dynasty, about the example they must set for the managerial staff who can be fired at will. I barely listened. When he had finished, I declared that my decision was irrevocable. He had tried to prevent my marriage; I had refused to give in and

I had won. He must understand that I had a stronger will than he gave me credit for. I finished with the phrase: 'You're very fond of Lena, aren't you?'

"He jumped as though bitten. 'What does she have to do with this?'

" 'In case you've forgotten, she's my wife. We want to be together, that's all.'

"I thought he turned slightly pale. 'Did she say that she wants you to give up your present job?'

" 'We have no need to speak in order to understand one another. I feel extremely close to Lena. You know as well as I how agreeable marriage can be. We suffer during such long separations. I shouldn't confess this to you, but man to man, I must tell you that making love to her is like—'

" 'Enough!' he shouted. Then he stood up; his voice had changed. 'I wouldn't dream of interfering in your marital affairs. Go to see Wolf tomorrow, tell him to show you our latest organizational chart, choose the post that suits you. You will act as deputy to the person who holds it. We will see in a year if the job pleases you.'

"Lars sat at his desk and used the telephone to call his secretary and tell her that he had a letter to dictate.

"I had won the first round. I now had to win over my wife. She was in the habit of working late, while my day ended at five-thirty P.M. I listened to Mozart or Bach while awaiting her return. I asked no questions, but tried to entertain and amuse her. It was certainly painful for her to know that I was at home waiting for her while Lars was exposing his philosophy to her in his office. She should have been the one who waited at home for me. She began to feel remorseful and arranged to return earlier. We ceased going to Storö for the weekend. I invented a thousand varied excursions: We went to visit archeological diggings, we took the boat to Copenhagen to see a show of contemporary paintings, et cetera. I tried to undermine my father's influence over Lena. All his life he had attracted everyone's attention; he was the center of the universe. He received his friends only to convert them to his way of thinking. He had even explained Shakespeare to a professor of English literature. He saw himself as a sun around which the planets revolved; the rest were only motes in his eyes. Lena tried to behave tenderly toward me, as though aware of the difficulties she had created.

"The political situation had begun to worry us. It was becoming evident that the Nazis were now trying to extend their power to cover all of Europe. They were demanding more space in which to expand. The victors of 1918 had humiliated, starved, and brought to despair those they had vanquished with so much difficulty. Lars had foreseen that a war economy would be established. He calculated Germany's resources, the formidable strength of a country hypnotized by such a magician as Hitler, who had mobilized his people's forces by nourishing them with illusions. He knew that France was weak, England insular, Italy opportunistic. He was certain that, to satisfy Germany's dreams of revenge, war would soon break out. He oriented the Group's activities on that basis, sensing that Sweden as a neutral country could furnish arms and equipment to the belligerents. The wood and steel industries were about to experience an unprecedented expansion. He foresaw what stocks would be necessary, what raw materials to buy. At our board meetings we discussed these perspectives, in which I could not bring myself to believe. Who would dare to sacrifice millions of men, to bleed Europe white, to destroy an equilibrium that had been so painfully established? I could not understand the madness of men. Unable, as always, to withstand his domination, Lena took my father's point of view.

"We savored the pleasant days of a mild and lovely September. I had bought a boat, taught Lena to sail, and we went on long outings, cruising among the islands. I was delighted to be alone with Lena, lost between the waves and the sky, as though no one else existed save the seagulls wheeling and diving overhead. We avoided any topics that might disturb the peace and serenity of our days together. If we thought of Lars, we never mentioned him. When I embraced Lena, tasting the salt on her lips, she no longer drew back, but seemed to accept me.

"She continued to be sweet and kind with me, saving her aggressiveness for the business affairs she handled. One of my clients told me that my wife had been intractable with him. He remarked that it must not be pleasant for me to live day in and day out with such a strong-minded woman. Sure of Lars's support, she spared no one. Such professional toughness helped dissipate her nervous tensions. I was content to profit from an armistice whose terms I didn't attempt to analyze. It seemed to me miraculous to have Lena with me every night; we spoke in the hushed voices of convalescents, discussing which film we should see, what color we should choose to paint the boat. Neither of us mentioned our work, so as to avoid any possibility of an argument.

"One day, as though she were telling me that she

was going to the store to buy some carrots, she announced that she had to travel to London to meet with a client, that my father considered the trip necessary. I was faced with a *fait accompli*.

" 'I won't let you go! I forbid it!' I cried.

"My anxiety, the anger I had suppressed during the preceding months, poured out. Fragile in her wispy nightdress, Lena looked at me without saying a word. I clenched my fists. I wanted desperately to shake her, to slap her, to stop her from making me suffer.

" 'You shan't go. I absolutely forbid it!' I shouted once more.

"She gazed thoughtfully at her nails and replied: 'Discuss it with your father, then.'

" 'My father can go to hell. I wish he'd drop dead! You don't really believe that I don't know that—' I yelled.

" 'That what?'

"I was afraid of the words I was going to pronounce, but I had to finish the phrase.

" 'What you and he are about!'

"Lena leaned back on her pillow, drew up the sheets and blankets to her chin, then turned toward me. She spoke like a judge addressing a jury.

" 'My poor Nils, you are really unbalanced when you talk like that. It's thanks to him that I've stayed with you. He has made it possible for me to lead a passionately interesting existence. Because of the responsibilities he has given me, I finally have the feeling that I really exist. It's to him that I owe my ability to be a proper wife to his son. Why do you complain so bitterly? This trip is part of my job. I refuse to obey you, in spite of your horrid insinuations.'

"She turned her back to me and then suddenly

cried out: 'You disgust me! I'm an adult woman; my work is as respectable and as important as that of a man! Why do you only see sex in all this?'

"I tried to apologize, to kiss her, to beg her pardon, but she pushed me away. Late into the night, I could hear her weeping.

"Winter passed. She went away twice. I didn't verify whether my father was in Stockholm or not. I wanted to leave Sweden for Australia or Canada, but I couldn't face parting from Lena, who I was certain would not follow me. My mother avoided me; I could never seem to find her alone so that we might talk. Carl and I became closer friends. He had just entered the Group after a training course in Germany. He detested my wife because of her influence over our father. She was working exceedingly hard, and since our last scene no longer bothered to spare my feelings. Once again she was coming home very late in the evening.

"Carl did not hesitate to inform me that Lena was now exercising influence outside the sphere of her position. She had just been named administrator of one of the companies, and was therefore participating in the board meetings of the Group.

" 'She's quite extraordinary,' said Carl. 'It's amazing how she manages to make you happy, perform a man's job, remain as beautiful as ever. How does she do it?'

"We were lunching together on smoked herring and bear steak. I hesitated, then replied: 'I allow her to be free; she knows how to organize her time.'

" 'You're not only an excellent husband, Nils, but also a good son,' he remarked, looking at me strangely. 'She spends time with Papa that she should be spending with you. And I'm not talking about her office hours, for which she is paid.'

" 'What do you mean, exactly?'

" 'What I'm driving at is that I'm interested in whether you approve of your wife's visits to the pavilion that Papa has built in the forest near Kiruna.'

" 'When did she go there?'

" 'Last week.'

" 'No, you're wrong. She was in Hamburg on business!'

" 'Ask her. Find out the truth,' he suggested.

"I couldn't possibly ask the secretaries. Who was I to believe—my father, my wife, or my brother? Should I divorce her? But I loved Lena. Was the truth as sordid as Carl wished me to believe? On Sunday, I took Lena to the forest. We walked silently over the pine cones. I sat down on a fallen tree trunk and she joined me. Some baby birds were calling to their mother. I tried to put together a sentence to form a question that I might ask her, when she placed her hand on my arm.

" 'Don't say anything, Nils, I beg of you. I'm very attached to you. If you wish, we can separate, but I prefer to remain with you. I need you. The life I'm leading suits me perfectly. I couldn't possibly stay home and take care of the house all day. Don't you understand that?'

" 'And if you had a child?' I asked.

" 'But I'm expecting one.'

" 'Lena!'

"She bent her head. I kissed her gently, but at the same time the serpent of doubt raised its head inside me."

Nils stopped. His hands were folded on his knees. He stared at Bernt, who had stood up.

"I'm sorry to interrupt you, but I feel as though I've opened a letter not addressed to me. My mother isn't here to defend herself. But may I ask you some questions?"

"As you wish."

"Are you certain that there was a physical relationship between your wife and your father?"

"Yes."

"I prefer not to hear any of the details. You swear to me that what you say is true?"

Nils sighed.

"Families such as ours, who are accustomed to living in the public eye, are in the habit of hiding their dirty linen. Passions and dramas are kept secret, never go beyond the walls of those houses hidden in a park and so admired by the passersby. We present ourselves to the world as a solid bloc, and whatever be the hatreds or disagreements which divide us, we are as one when we face our staff or our stockholders. We are the royal family—a monarchy. I kept my doubts and my fears to myself. Your birth was a joy to everyone, especially to old Lars, who saw in you his assurance of an heir to succeed him in the business. My cowardice, an instinct to save what could be saved, a sense of duty, my reluctance to destroy my home, kept me from trying to find out the truth. I waited until you were almost two years old before I drove to the pavilion deep in the midst of the forest of Kiruna where, Carl had told me, they were in the habit of meeting. I recognized my father's Bentley in the courtyard. I entered the house. Lena's red coat was thrown over a chair. I had crossed over the borderline to that side leading to the kingdom of shadows and ghosts, where the birds wake the dead and put to sleep the living. I raced back to Stockholm like a madman. Though I wished desperately to disappear beyond recall, to suffer no longer, the life force was too strong within me, and I arrived safely."

"Then, the following Sunday, you invited Mama to go out on the boat with you?"

"Yes, but how did you know that?"

"The investigation was suppressed, the matter was hushed up. The family's influence saw to it that her death was called 'drowned by accident.' No one suspected the truth save Grandfather. He understood that you had discovered his liaison with Lena. You had it out with him. What did he say to you?"

"That he would never forgive me. He had the superb gift of camouflaging his destructiveness. I told him that I was leaving. I meant to bring you here with me. Mama had given me this place. I was going to move into it. He avoided my eyes and contemplated his hands, which were covered with the brown spots of old age. If he could have strangled me, his own son, I believe that he would have done so. His hands were clenched, but he controlled himself. I could feel the intensity of his disgust as he shouted out to me to leave and never return. Then he stood up, his eyes sunken, and quietly murmured: 'Leave me my son. Bernt is mine.' I ran. Not only had he stolen my wife, but also my child. I threw my clothes into suitcases and left without entering the bedroom where you were sleeping. If you had smiled at me, perhaps I would not have had the courage to leave you. I asked my mother to send my furniture here and to sell the apartment."

Bernt strode up and down like a caged animal. The snow began to fall as he gazed out the window.

"Did you believe him?"

Nils seemed surprised.

"Why would he have risked scandal with such a lie?"

Bernt fell into a tapestried armchair.

"I disagree with you. Grandfather felt a passion for my mother that was all the more violent for being his last. His prestige, his personality, his amorality, his cleverness had won her over. No one ever resisted him, neither clients nor employees nor members of the government nor women. Why would she have refused to give in to his desires? He accepted the fact that he must leave her to you officially and content himself with seeing her only when they could snatch stolen moments together. When you deprived him of her—forever—he tried to avenge himself. He hated you. He found a way to wound you mortally. Who can be sure of a paternity? You loved your wife; you proved that. There is more chance that I am your son rather than his. He was almost sixty."

"That's your opinion. In any case, I haven't thought about it for years. I feel no responsibility for you, no attachment to you. You were raised by your grandfather, not by me."

"Is that why you agreed to let Carl go ahead with instituting changes in the setup of the Group?"

Nils replied in a disillusioned voice: "You know, I'm no longer really involved with all that."

Bernt drew his chair closer.

"Whether you wish it to be so or not, your shares give you the power to control the final decision. Aren't you content with the way I've been running things? Haven't you seen the profits listed on the last balance sheet? What do you have to reproach me for?"

"Nothing, except that you are too self-confident, arrogant, and that you refuse to listen to anyone. You're like my father. You mean to invest in unproven industries; this alarms Carl and your cousins."

Bernt defended his position. Within twenty years, new industries devoted to the exploitation of the oceans were going to spring up, since the seas were rich in oil, gas, diamonds, uranium, tin. Cities would be built under the waves. Computers would be used in homes the way telephones were today. Radios, worn like bracelets, would use the heat produced by the body to transmit messages. Using electronic means, medicine would replace faltering organs with artificial anatomical parts. Large industries would be built to carry out biological reconstruction. Human thought would feed directly into the memory of a computer, which would then make mechanical decisions. It was essential that the Group prepare for such eventualities.

Nils remained cold and distant. His voice fell like the sharp blade of a guillotine:

"It is not a question of decisions about the future, but about you yourself. It seems that you refuse to listen to the opinions of the administrators and directors. It would be wiser to cede your place to your uncle for a while. It is healthy, believe me, to become a member of the rank and file. You will discover the joys of discipline."

"But that's impossible, idiotic! Carl is incapable of running the business!"

"You may think that, but my decision is final,

Bernt. I'm closer to my brother than to you. You must give in before the decision of the majority. You can, if you profit from this period of reflection, become president of the Group again when Carl reaches the age of retirement. You have been ridiculously spoiled by my father, who made you believe that you belonged to an elite race and therefore were absolved from having ever to justify yourself. You have believed you were superman. You must learn to compromise, to adjust, to belong to a team—and that will do you worlds of good."

He spoke like the father that he no longer was. Bernt's cup was full. It was impossible to remain in this house any longer. To accept the hospitality of a man who had twice rejected him seemed more than he could bear. He was going to be forced to confront public opinion, to read spiteful commentaries in the newspapers that would place in doubt his management, raise suspicions, and throw out vile insinuations. Why were children obliged to pay for their parents' mistakes? For how many generations did a curse endure? He was to be punished, though his only sin was that of being Lena's son.

Bernt looked at his watch.

"I'm sorry, but I must go. My plane leaves in an hour. Present my excuses to your wife. Explain to her that I have an urgent appointment."

Nils stood up. He seemed saddened.

"I hope that you're not angry with me for having disclosed those old secrets to you. I could have kept silent, but I thought that you deserved to know the truth at your age."

Nils had enjoyed a certain pleasure in wounding Bernt and a rather subtle satisfaction in causing his public humiliation by agreeing to his removal from office, though he could have prevented it.

"You're sure that you don't want to stay and dine with us?"

"I prefer to return to Stockholm."

They walked to the door in silence. Bernt took his coat and scarf.

"When will I be notified of the terms and conditions of the administrative changes?" he asked.

"Speak to Carl. Everything will turn out for the best. It only involves a change of posts. We need you in the Group."

Bernt looked at the man who had once been his father, opened his mouth, then closed it quickly, shook his head and disappeared into the dark night filled with snow flurries. For him no hope remained.

VII

BERNT WAS DISTRESSED BY THE ABSURDITY OF THE SITUA-
tion. Usually he was able to find a solution to the
most seemingly insurmountable problems, but this
time the trap had snapped shut and, however incredi-
ble it might be, he himself was the victim of its iron
jaws. How was he to free himself?

The airline hostess approached and asked if he
would like some coffee or akvavit. He declined to
have either. Bernt no longer recognized himself. He
wished that he could surrender, could float uncaring
as seagulls on the winds' currents. He tried to brush
aside the memory of Nils's revelations and to concentrate on his fears for the future—not for himself but
for those who had trusted him, were dedicated to
him. How would Bo, Erik, Jan, Albert, and the others
react to the news of his departure? A dozen or so
years spent in managing and controlling a group of

men had given him an understanding of the fundamental insecurity of all employees, an insecurity that
could at a moment's notice turn the best of them into
cowards and traitors. They asked for news of Ingrid
and the children, remembered his birthday, avoided
disagreeing with him too hotly so as not to risk his
displeasure. Such servile men would certainly obey
the orders of the new management, and now it would
be Carl who would benefit from their smiles, their patience, their capacity for hard work. Knowing that
they would never be in a position to make important
decisions, that they were at the mercy of an employer
who could fire them from one day to the next despite
their devotion to duty, they would sell their souls to
the owners of the Group—whoever they might be.
Otto was different. He would prefer to follow his
chief rather than come to terms with those who had
removed him from office.

Bernt doted on his men with a jealous, possessive
affection. They belonged to him. He had formed
them, using old Lars's technique. He knew and appreciated them better than did his cousins. The members
of his personal staff had become experts whose reputation had earned them job offers from rival companies, which until now they had refused. What would
become of them? The Group would be damaged by
the absence of a firm hand at its wheel. Carl did not
possess that fire which makes men lucky and successful in their business dealings. The stock would fall in
value. Their competitors would seize the opportunity
to steal away Erik, Bo, Albert, and Jan by offering
them salaries higher than they were worth.

Bernt waved to the air hostess and ordered a double whiskey on the rocks.

Lars must be turning in his grave! He had detected in Bernt the best material in the family, had accorded more attention to his education than he had to that of his sons, had been determined to prepare his heir to meet his responsibilities. And here was his grandson at thirty-nine, strong, at the height of his powers, with experience allied to youthful vigor, being dismissed from the leadership of the Group, *his* Group!

He drank his whiskey down at one gulp, feeling vulnerable as a newborn child, naked as he would be at the hour of his death, as he constructed hypotheses and envisaged the future in the light of what he had just learned from Nils. The solution depended on him alone. He had always believed that all problems contained with them their own answer, waiting only to be discovered. But the shock administered to him by his family had stripped him of every reflex, of his very life force. He saw himself ill-at-ease with his father, a glass in his hands, watching the flames rising from the half-burned log. The truth had hit him squarely in the face. He could still hear himself asking:

"Are you sure that there was a physical tie between them?"

And Nils, avoiding his eyes as he answered, "Yes."

He recalled the photograph of Lena in a muslin dress with a rose at the waist, her hair tied back with a ribbon. Lars had obviously decided to take her as soon as he had laid eyes on her. His son represented an obstacle of no more consequence than an insect. How could that great industrial giant have given in to so primitive a temptation? He should have controlled his impulses, waited for another distraction to replace his desire for Lena. Having revealed such a cardinal weakness, how had he dared assume the right to lecture others on morality? The problem had not been a simple one: The last gasp of passion in a man's life is the most painful. Had the old pirate struggled against his own nature? Probably not. His personality was so powerful that he had undoubtedly seduced his son's fiancée without giving it a thought.

She had recognized in him a desirable master. Why had she not been honest enough to give up Nils when she realized that she had become fascinated by his father? Had she tried to disguise that attraction? Had she persuaded herself that, given the difference in their ages, he could not possibly be a dangerous obstacle to her marital happiness? She had perhaps believed that she really loved Nils, whose adoration and tenderness promised a marriage of safety and harmony. She had been aware of her future father-in-law's reputation, his genius. Imagination prepares the ground for love; the eruption of that sacred giant into her life took a place in her thoughts much larger than that of the young, inexperienced man who had asked her to share his life. Lena had heard his step on the terrace, causing those around the table in the garden to fall silent. When for the first time she had met his eyes, the impact had been so intense that she had turned her head away for a moment. In that instant they had become accomplices. In that flicker of an eyelid he had accepted her, raised her to his level. She had been the only person who had not feared him, because she had understood him perfectly.

During their long rides together, when he had tied their horses to the branch of a birch tree, he had told her that he needed her, that his power had condemned him to solitude, that she was the only person with whom he could possibly communicate. All very well to say that she should not have listened to him: she had felt as vulnerable as a captive bird. She had loved his broad shoulders, his piercing glance, his absence of self-consciousness or doubt, his vigor, his surprising tenderness. Had they discussed her approaching marriage? In order to protect their budding passion as one would protect a child, they had with a common accord limited the number of their meetings. No one had noticed anything. Nils had adored his fiancée and had been proud to see that Lars approved of his choice. How could she have broken with him? Her father had encouraged her to enter into that great Swedish dynasty. She had received a lovely diamond ring, earrings, and a clip; a reception attended by a thousand people, including the prime minister, had been given in her honor in the family's great house. She had allowed herself to be carried away by a whirlwind whose end result had been a honeymoon with Nils whom she loved like a brother, a voyage financed by Lars, the sight of whom made her tremble with suppressed passion.

One morning before their marriage, Nils had told her that his father had capriciously decided to oppose their union but that he, Nils, was determined to proceed against all opposition. Without telling her fiancé, she had called Lars, who had ordered his secretary to say that he was in conference and could not be disturbed. She had then sent him a note, insisting that she must speak with him. The reply had been a bouquet of roses accompanied by an unsigned message: "I don't have the courage." Several days later, Nils informed her that his father had given in and that they were free to marry.

After their marriage, Lena lost contact with Lars. Her days were occupied in furnishing the apartment and trying to make Nils happy. In the autumn she was surprised to learn that her husband was going to be away a great deal on business in the Orient. It was not easy to be the heir to a dynasty, he had explained; the survival of the Group depended on its officers fulfilling their responsibilities. Lena did not argue. She found it difficult to tolerate solitude, and while her husband was away she fell into the habit of spending her evenings with her in-laws. When Lars offered her a job with him, on the basis of her degree in political economy, she accepted with delight and without taking thought of how little her professional qualifications had equipped her for the position her father-in-law proposed. She loved being active, and as she assisted in preparing the president's strategy, in sharing his struggles and then his victories, the admiration that she felt for him grew. Professional coexistence weaves a special bond: For the man and woman who work side by side eight hours a day, who share the same risks and tremble at the same fears, the celebration of their mutual success has a particular sweetness.

When her husband returned two years later, Lena realized that her marriage had been a mistake. His conversation bored her and she was exasperated by his physical demands. During a walk with Lars on the beach at Storö, while he spoke to her of a business problem, she strode along with her hands clenched into fists in the pockets of her raincoat, the heels of her boots digging furiously into the sand, as she stared distractedly at the seagulls flying three or four hundred meters above their heads. Her father-in-law stopped, astonished at her inattention.

"But Lena, you haven't heard a word I've said!"

The wind disheveled her hair. She raised her face to his.

"I've been wondering why gulls fly fifteen to thirty thousand kilometers just to face hunger, danger, and exhaustion."

Lars stared at her, and her head spun. He took her in his arms, holding her so tightly that she felt her bones might break.

"They fly from pole to pole, they leave comfort and security to confront unknown perils, perhaps death, Lena, because of an irresistible compulsion called love."

As he kissed her, she realized that she had never before in her life received a kiss.

She had been led by Lars beyond the point of madness. How could she tell her husband and destroy her marriage? She waited, hoping that circumstances would present some clue as to what path she should follow. Lars had no intention of clarifying the situation. Given his position, he could not afford a scandal. They stole their moments together discreetly and with care not to disturb the basic structure of their lives. Brevity made their meetings all the sweeter; afterward, at night, she lay sleepless beside Nils, reliving every passionate instant she had spent with his father. But then destiny decided that she could no longer cheat with impunity—she became pregnant. After Bernt's birth, she gave no sign that she loved her son, but handed him over to the care of a nurse and went back to work with Lars. And so life went on until her mysterious fall from the boat into the sea. Had Nils

become angry, had he struck her? If she had fallen
overboard by accident, he might have saved her. Had
she struggled against the icy water and pleaded with
him to rescue her? Had he coldly watched her lose
her battle with the breaking seas, and then sailed
away in the opposite direction? Bernt hid his head in
his hands. He suspected that Lena had been too fragile to live such an impossible love and had chosen of
her own free will to disappear from the world of the
living.

The plane was flying over the forest. He no longer
felt the least desire to see again the man whom until
now he had considered to be his father. He felt like
an orphan. Whose son was he? The doubt would torment him until the end of his life.

After Lena's burial, Nils had taken refuge in his
forest retreat to wait for the wound to heal. Although
he had controlled the resentment he felt toward Bernt
for his very existence, he had never been able, during
his annual or semiannual visits to the boy, to bring
himself to attempt a close acquaintance with him. He
undoubtedly saw in his son the symbol of his own
misfortune. The years had passed. Bernt was, of
course, bewildered by his father's indifference. After
Lars's death, instead of moving into the family house
or his son's home, Nils chose to live in a hotel. He
showed no sorrow at the funeral, while Carl, who had
always been the unsentimental one, seemed very af-
fected by his father's passing and somberly helped his
mother to receive the condolences of their innumerable relatives and acquaintances. That evening, using
fatigue as a pretext, Nils had refused to dine with his
son. The next day they met at the notary public's office to hear the will read, and learned that Bernt was

the heir. The house and the impressionist paintings belonged to him, as did the island of Storö, with the provision that his grandmother live there until her death. When the lawyer read the paragraph in which Lars praised his grandson's intelligence and talent and stated that he was to be his successor, Carl had thrown him a look brimming with hatred; Nils had appeared aloof and unconcerned. Bernt had not been able to hide his embarrassment. Ten years later, Carl and Nils were making him pay with compound interest for that humiliation by divesting him publicly of his responsibilities. The brothers considered him an awkward appendage to the family. The child of an adventuress, the favorite son who resembled their sire so much more than they.

Who would guess the truth, who would understand that he, Bernt, was the victim of open warfare, of a settlement of accounts, dreamed of by its instigators since his birth? The law of silence would prevail. No one, least of all himself, would dare sully the family legend, that myth which must remain intact. He could never tell Ingrid or the children what he had learned on his visit to Nils. They would believe that he had committed a professional error which, as is usual in such cases, would be concealed by the new directors of the Group. Nothing is more changeable than public opinion. Those who had respected Bernt's character, his prudence, the rapidity of his decisions, the rising profits evidenced by his balance sheets, would now be persuaded that he was frivolous and inconsequential. The image that he had projected for a dozen years would be demolished as soon as his removal from office was made official. He had no way to justify himself; he would be condemned without

trial. Carl and his sons, wearing hypocritical Chesh-
ire-cat smiles, would hide behind professional secrecy,
would refuse to discuss the matter, would change the
subject and hasten to avail themselves of that power
of decision which had belonged to Bernt alone. Rumors, exaggerated in some quarters by envy, in others
by imagination, would reach the editorial offices of the
newspapers. What could he reply to the reporters
when they pressed him for answers?

He quickly swallowed a second glass of whiskey.
Heretofore, when he had been surrounded by danger,
had felt the dragon's breath scorching the grass close
on his heels, he had been able to keep calm and examine the situation as if he himself were not involved.
But he had never before felt so threatened; he had
sacrificed his private life, his artistic gifts, his desire
to roam the world to the Group. He had been living
proof of the falsity of the dictum, "The first generates
creates, the second conserves, the third squanders." It
was intolerable, impossible, that they were going to
throw him out, to annul Lars's mandate. He would
see the best lawyer in Stockholm. He would defend
himself in the courts, if need be. He must try to make
a deal with his uncle Carl, although chances for
success were slim. He would telephone the next day.
Carl would probably ask him to come to his office,
which was located in another section of town, so as to
make Bernt understand that he, Carl, was now the
master, that the wheel had turned.

The plane began its descent. He hadn't the courage
to face dining with Ingrid in the peaceful house, to
lie, to invent stories about his conversation with Nils.
His wife would not be worried if he did not return
that evening, because she had expected him to spend

the night with his father. He found it indispensable to enjoy a reprieve before facing his family or his business companions. He needed time to think, to become accustomed to the strange pangs of anguish that were gnawing at his vitals. He who had been so dynamic, so confident of the future, now discovered himself to be a suffering, sore, doubting, mutilated animal. He did not know for certain from whose loins he had sprung, only that he had been born of a young woman abandoned to the violence of the icy seas.

The plane had landed. Bernt followed the other passengers down the ramp into the cold night. Everyone was in a hurry to regain the warmth of their homes—all save Bernt. He passed by a newspaper stand and, after a mechanical glance at the headlines, directed his steps to a telephone and dialed.

"Hello."

He recognized the husky voice. He had been right to call. Luck had not really deserted him.

"I'm just back from a trip." He paused. "It's an ungodly hour, I know."

Ulla laughed.

"May I see you for a moment, if you're not busy? I'd like to talk with you."

He sensed her hesitation, and asked: "Are you with friends?"

"No. I was working on a report that I must finish."

"Could you take the time to meet me at a restaurant?"

"Why don't you come here instead? You have my address. If you're hungry, I'll make some sandwiches. It's such a cold night; I don't really want to go out."

Bernt agreed and hung up. The bird of prey that had gripped him in its talons, that had been on the point of ripping into his entrails, flapped up and away, and, for the first time that day, he breathed deeply and felt suddenly relaxed, almost exultant, nearly serene. As his taxi drove off, he told himself that the gods had not yet abandoned him.

VIII

THE TAXI DROVE TOWARD THE NEW HIGH-INCOME SEC-
tion of Stockholm, with its ultramodern apartment
buildings. Although a millionaire many times over,
Ulla's father had not given her a dowry; she worked
for his company and her husband was a trial lawyer.
Bernt was apprehensive about her reaction to his sudden visit. He wondered how long she would permit
him to stay, and whether later he would telephone for
a taxi and spend the night at the Intercontinental Hotel. He paid the driver and entered the building. Before the mirror in the elevator he straightened his tie
and, astonished at how weary his face looked, tried to
assume a lighthearted expression. Her door was ajar.
He entered the hallway carpeted in white, hung with
African totems and masks and furnished with two ancient chests.

Ulla, in a red turtleneck sweater and blue velvet

127

trousers, looked so gay, so pleased to see him, that he felt reassured, delighted that he had obeyed his instincts. He had felt the need of being comforted and here she was waiting for him, even more desirable than he had remembered.

He followed her into the kitchen and sat on a stool while she prepared a supper for him of smoked herring and fruit salad. They talked inconsequentially of this and that, and when his tray was ready, carried it into a living room whose monochromatic white was brightened and warmed by blue and orange cushions, innumerable abstract paintings in violent tones, and a colorful Calder mobile suspended from the ceiling. Bernt went to the bay window; the open curtains revealed a view of an estuary in which rectangles of light from a skyscraper opposite were reflected. A barge carrying sand slipped by, leaving gleaming waves in its wake. Standing next to him, Ulla murmured:

"Perhaps it's because I was born under the sign of the Fishes, but I could watch the sea forever. Some boats carrying logs lie so deep in the water that their hulls are almost submerged, others carry pyramids of gravel, cement, barrels, God knows what! Before Christmas, I saw a tugboat hauling a barge covered with pine trees."

She seemed different from the self-assured young woman whom he had received in his office.

"If I dared, I'd swim out to sea, then come back against the current. Haven't you ever felt like doing that?"

As he was about to answer, she tugged at his arm:

"Come and eat! You must be starving!"

Bernt sat on the sofa and began with the delicious herring.

"I'm ashamed of having broken in on you like this."

"Don't be so conventional! Tell me instead what you've discovered about your uncle's plans."

He felt in no mood to discuss business affairs yet. He was curious about her life. Did she work all day long every day in her father's office? Christer Linders owned an enormous fleet of oil tankers, and Ulla took her job with her father very seriously. In Sweden, the idea that a woman should be materially dependent on her husband does not exist. Ulla behaved toward hers as an associate, an equal. What was the lawyer like? Bernt felt a pang of jealousy.

"I'm curious about your husband."

"Daniel? At thirty he's still very athletic. If there's enough snow, he leaves the house at seven in the morning to ski near here. He comes back with his shirt wringing wet. Before he takes his shower, he puts on the record player and whistles the theme of the symphony he has chosen while the water runs."

"Where is he now?"

"In Africa. He's due back on May first."

She put on the record player and the adagio movement of Mozart's concerto for clarinet burst forth. Bernt was transported into the forest near Kiruna where he loved to walk in hunting boots among the giant trees, ending up at the sacrificial stone of the ancients at the base of the huge oak, whose wreathed branches evoked a magic dating from antiquity.

Ulla was silent, her green eyes inscrutable as emeralds. When the movement had ended, she carried the tray to the kitchen, and on returning drew a pouf up to the sofa.

"Would you like to talk about our business now?"

When he shook his head, she seemed disappointed.
She was totally different from Donatella, who had
been too eminently feminine to work at a profession.
Stretched out on his bed in Siena, his arms folded
beneath his head, he had loved to look at her seated
before her dressing table, plucking her eyebrows,
curling her lashes, or massaging her neck with cream.
Though barely thirty, she had already been afraid of
getting old. Her beauty, her youth had been her only
trumps. She had suffered because she was sterile;
bearing children was more important in Italy than in
Sweden. Love reassured her, proved to her that her
powers of seduction remained intact. Helpless before
an existence that she had not chosen of her own free
will, having passed at nineteen from the hands of her
father into those of a husband, knowing that because
she was incapable of living alone she would never
leave him, Donatella had been a victim, while Ulla
brandished aloft the banner of freedom. So long as
her husband suited her, she would share his life; the
day a passionate love captured her heart, she would
leave to follow the man who had kindled it.

She insisted that Bernt discuss the business situation with her. He sighed and said:

"Your intuition was right. It's a family problem. My
father has been retired for years; he lives off in the
woods among eagles and bears, and is not only ill-in-
formed about what is going on, but doesn't care.
Without informing me of his intentions, my uncle
Carl went to see him and talked him into backing him
in a plan to take over the presidency of the Group.
Out of boredom, lethargy, or stubbornness, my father
refuses to change his mind. We are a democratic out-

fit; Carl will be named president at the next general meeting!"

She studied his face carefully.

"What are you going to do?"

"It's not in my nature to give in, but if the arbitrator declares that I've lost, I shall yield. I care too much about sparing our Group to sow discord among my associates. A business team draws its dynamism from a well of common faith. Each cell must feel responsible for the collective success. In the past when we've had difficult moments, I always explained to my men what I expected of them, how they could help me. I made sure that they understood our long-term aims. And the result was that I obtained total dedication and we won most battles. Afterward, we would drink together to our victory."

"Didn't you ever encounter any obstacles?" she asked, moving from the pouf to sit beside him on the sofa.

He shook his head.

"So far as I can remember, no. I generally considered myself responsible for my failures; I overcame them or made the best of them. But this time I haven't entirely grasped the situation; therefore, I haven't been able to come to terms with it. Perhaps the blow is too recent."

He was still in a state of shock; like the survivor of an accident, he as yet felt no pain. Later he would count his wounds, some of which could never heal—Lena with her lover in the lodge at Kiruna—Lena, a dark shadow sinking beneath the waves—vertigo at the realization that he did not know whose son he was. Bernt put his arm around Ulla. He knew so little about her!

"What is your mother like, Ulla?"

She smiled.

"Very pretty. Dark-haired with blue eyes. In her spare time she writes music. My brother and I used to hide behind the curtains and listen to her playing the piano."

"And does your father love her?"

"He has had mistresses, but she never knew about them. She's so naïve! She sees him still with the eyes of a sixteen-year-old. He's always been extremely attached to her. When we were children as they talked about their early days together, we felt as though we were being indiscreet, because they always seemed so very close to each other, which somehow shut out the rest of the world."

Bernt ran his fingers through Ulla's hair. There was something unattainable about her. She knew more about her father's business dealings than did her brother and, unlike her mother, who was content to rule over her household like a good wife, to take care of her children, to compose music, Ulla was fascinated by politics, economics, finance, and the oil business, and determined to be independent.

"Where did you meet your husband?"

She drew away.

"In London. I was about to marry an Englishman, but was hesitating as I didn't want to leave my family. Daniel fell in love with me and brought me back to Stockholm with him. I was twenty-three and wanted to settle down. I had no reason to refuse him."

Ulla drew her strength from her ties with her family, whereas Bernt's image of his father was of

Nils cutting his putative son's wrists and then waiting to see his lifeblood ebb away. Because Bernt presided over one of the most powerful industrial and banking groups in Europe, because he had demonstrated such vigilance, fortitude, and self-command, they believed that he could stand anything. No one bothered to find out what lay beneath his calm exterior. A whirlwind of questions without answers swirled about him. What had he done to make them hate him so? Why had Lena accepted the impossible? Why are children responsible for their parents' errors? Fragments of quotations from the Bible ran through his head.

Ulla leaned slightly upon him. He breathed in her perfume; through his jacket he felt the warmth of her body.

"How long have you been married?" she asked.

"Twelve years."

"Have you often been unfaithful to your wife?"

"Not yet."

She looked surprised. It was obvious that he was deeply interested in women, that he appreciated their company, their conversation, their beauty. Simultaneously they burst out laughing. They were beginning to be aware that they shared a certain complicity, that they were becoming far more intimate than they had consciously anticipated. Dangerous Ulla! She was the sort of beautiful and intelligent woman who gives a tired man sustenance, who restores his serenity. He was amazed that she had agreed to let him come. Had she understood that he was suffering and needed her help?

The future threw its shadow over the present. Perhaps it was better that he shepherd his strength for the storm that he must face, and not become entangled sentimentally. He could not easily lie to Ingrid, invent official dinners and business trips in order to explain his absences. Also, it was obviously not in Ulla's nature to play second fiddle. She was honest; she would insist that their relationship be out in the open. Bernt was in the habit of concentrating his energies on his work, infusing it with all his vigor and imagination, of living, so far as his inner life was concerned, in a state of hibernation. Once a week he would cross over the space separating the twin beds, and, after ten minutes with his wife, his duty accomplished, he would return to his own bed to fall asleep immediately. Ingrid never complained. She undoubtedly believed that the novelists' lyrical descriptions of lovemaking were the product of their excessive imaginations, of their habit of embellishing reality and giving it the color of their dreams. She would never have spoken with her friends about such intimate subjects as love and sex, and thus had no way of finding out the truth. She was satisfied with what she imagined to be the common lot; she had no desire to break any barriers and to discover the unknown.

As Ulla raised her eyes to his, he drew her to him and crushed her lips beneath his own. Then, in an effort at self-control, he drew away.

"I must go, Ulla," he murmured. "May I see you again, soon?"

Her cool green eyes were fixed unwaveringly upon his face, as though she wished to take possession of him.

Making a supreme effort to tear himself away from the enchantment that he felt stealing over him, he sprang to his feet, strode to the hallway and snatched up his coat and briefcase. His hand was on the door to the corridor when a cry stopped him:

"Stay!"

IX

THEY SLEPT ENTWINED IN THE NARROW BED. BERNT HAD
been surprised by the intensity of his ardor. Ulla's
body had aroused him from a long torpor, awakened
a sensual vigor that he had thought he no longer
possessed. But was his newfound serenity a mirage?
After all, he knew so little about her, apart from the
violence of her passion for him. She lay with her head
thrown back, her lips half open, looking completely
vulnerable. In her sleep, she tossed and turned as
though defending herself against some fearful adversary in her dreams. What phantom haunted her, what
spectres disturbed her inner peace? Perhaps she used
desire as a drug. Like many another twenty-five-
year-old of her day, she had undoubtedly taken a
lover at sixteen and been disappointed, concluding
very likely that physical love had been overestimated.
But she would have continued, changed lovers as

naturally as one changes partners at a ball. He imagined that she was innocent of the idea of possession; she would, of course, smile at pangs of jealousy, that madness described in books and films. Since early childhood, her admiration had been centered on her father, an authoritarian Viking who had formed her with no care for the damage he might cause her. He belonged to the same race as Lars, who had gratified his passions without thought for the consequences. How had Lars dared behave as he had? Bernt was paying dearly for the old pirate's casual attitude. He could well understand Carl. It was natural that his rather ugly, slightly lame uncle should hate a handsome, athletic man like his nephew. There is a rule in chess that the adversary must be hated, since understanding of the enemy's motives leads to sympathy and weakens one's defenses. Already the conversation with his father was beginning to seem less crucial.

Bernt ran his fingers lightly over Ulla's body and thought how pleasant it would be to give her a child. She had filled him with such rapture that he had felt immortal. But how could he presume to be safe from the ravages of time, when photographs in family albums reveal so clearly evidence to the contrary? The camera, unlike the eye, discerns almost before the fact the incipient double chin, the hollowing cheek, the withering eyelid, all that the passing years accomplish as they sap our very foundations.

Bernt drew Ulla, limp and unresisting, to him. They embraced in the calm of enchantment, the past forgotten, the future abolished. An intoxicated stupor of happiness possessed him, warm and delicious. Yet he knew with dreadful certainty that it must end.

Like a man on the eve of his execution, he foresaw the black future.

An hour later he rose, showered and dressed. Ulla remained in bed, watching his every move.

"Why are you leaving?"

"I'm going to take a room at the Hotel Intercontinental to rest and read the morning papers. I'll be at my office by nine o'clock."

Ulla hesitated, then asked:

"And when will you go home?"

"This evening."

He preferred not to think of Ingrid with her blond chignon, her clear soap-and-water complexion, her simple, innocent questions. He would avoid being alone with her, would use the children to create a diversion. While Ulla was imagining their next meeting, Bernt was erasing all sensual and tender memories in preparation for the difficulties of the coming day.

As he leaned down to kiss her good-bye, Ulla threw her arms around his neck:

"Don't go, Bernt! I want to know how you intend to deal with your uncle, what decisions you have made. You aren't the sort to give in under pressure, are you?"

Her insistence annoyed him. He disengaged himself from her embrace, placed a finger on her lips and slipped out of the room.

At the hotel, he ran a bath that dissipated his fatigue, and pondered the problem of negotiating his departure under the best conditions. Should he suggest that they divide the empire between them? Should he invite Carl to lunch?

He ordered a large breakfast—dried fish, scrambled

eggs, toast, coffee. Where was his energy, his strength of character? He was obsessed with the secret pact between his father and his uncle, an agreement made at his expense. How could he escape from the net closing around him? His exhausted mind left him with only one certitude—that there was no answer. He tried to concentrate on the newspapers. Japan was going to raise its export prices. They had decided to help China enter the industrial age. The Japanese were a stoic race; they had enough discipline to export their products and, if necessary, go without at home. They were going to conquer the planet with their miniature calculators, their transistors, their cameras, their watches, their small machine tools, their computers. They were investing their newly won fortunes in works of art from all over the world; the second step would be a buildup of offensive armaments. Japan would soon have its own nuclear force as well as a powerful standing army. Bernt shook his head. Of what use was it to detect the signs of impending international conflict if he was not even capable of discerning what his own future was to be?

He swallowed a second cup of coffee and grimly envisaged the future: Carl ringing his office and asking him to study a report on the recent elections in East Germany; himself composing and submitting for Carl's approval a memorandum dealing with future markets; being obliged to ask for Carl's authorization before engaging in any interesting business enterprises. What would he look like in the eyes of his old associates? As to the directors of rival companies, whom he would meet at his club or during international meetings, he preferred not to dwell on the prospect of their smiles and innuendoes.

What should he do? To whom could he turn? He decided to telephone Ingrid; it was eight o'clock in the morning. She answered in a sleepy voice:

"Oh, it's you! When did you get back?"

He was surprised by her coolness. Usually she was more amiable.

"A few minutes ago. Anything new at home?"

"Viveca has been impossible. I wonder if we shouldn't send her off to boarding school."

"We'll discuss that this evening. I have a lot of work to do, and will probably be home late."

He could get along without Ulla. Her life lay elsewhere than in his arms. In thirty years, Ulla would have been forgotten; he would walk with his wife in the gardens at Storö, while their grandchildren gambolled about them.

Overnight the aspect of his office seemed to him to have changed; the pleasure that he took on entering it each morning had been destroyed. The room now seemed too vast because of his new loss of faith in himself. He was like a pastor who, in the process of delivering a sermon, asks himself what meaning the liturgy can possibly hold. His joy, his enthusaism, his self-esteem had disappeared. Everything to which he had devoted his energy, his imagination, his strength was about to be legally torn from him. And he would be expected to accept his removal calmly and with grace. When the time came for him to hand over the keys to his safe to Carl, during the ceremony that would take place to celebrate the passing of power from one to the other—a barbarous rite to which he must submit—every eye would be on his face.

Depressed by such musings, Bernt rang for his secretary.

Margret arrived wearing her eternal shapeless gray flannel dress, her hair tied back severely in a bun, her glasses set firmly on her nose, her steno pad in hand. She was forty-five, a spinster, and as devoted as a pet dog whose only pleasure lies in the approbation of its master. She was at the opposite pole from those nubile twenty-year olds in seductive tight sweaters with hair swinging loose to their shoulders pictured in ads for temporary office workers. They resembled Ulla! He felt his belly contract. How had he thought that he could forget the night he had spent with her, the youth she had restored to him?

"Was your trip successful, sir?"

He stared at Margret uncomprehendingly.

"You met with your father . . ."

Bernt replied distantly: "Thank you. Are you ready? Take a letter to Ake Halfstrom, president of the U.J.S. Steelworkers, Sveavagen 13. 'My dear friend . . .'"

When he had dictated a dozen letters, Margret broke in:

"Otto asked to see you, sir. He has a message from the prime minister."

"Why didn't you tell me earlier? Call him in immediately."

He felt comforted by the sight of the faithful Otto, who informed him that the prime minister had called to invite Ingrid and Bernt to dinner the following month. He wished to see Bernt beforehand, and had suggested 6:30 P.M. the following day.

Bernt told Margret to cancel a meeting he had scheduled for that hour, and turned to Otto.

"What does he want?"

"Probably he's going to tell you about a financial

move he has in mind before he gives it to the newspapers for publication."

"Otto, I must talk to you. Have you heard anything about a change in the top echelon of our Group?"

"Yes, sir."

"What are they saying?"

For the past week, Otto revealed, gossip had been circulating through the offices. The heirs of the old president, it seemed, were contesting the arrangements he had made before his death, arguing that age and excessive influence wielded over him by his grandson had caused him to change his will.

"Why didn't you tell me all this before?"

"Your time is too precious, sir. It seemed ridiculous to spend it on such nonsense! Usually such talk means nothing."

"That isn't the case here, alas."

Otto remained impassive. Only his sparkling eyes revealed his interest.

Bernt took a deep breath.

"I don't wish to go into details, but I may be forced to leave. I will make sure, however, that you and the others have your future assured. I'll see to it that they don't touch you. As for me, I don't know what lies ahead. I've made no decisions. I must consult with my uncle, who will probably succeed me."

Otto, deeply moved, said softly: "Only your future concerns me at the moment, sir."

"Otto, I shall be forty this year. I came to work here immediately after graduating from Harvard. I've been a kind of prisoner ever since. I've forgotten such pleasures as leafing through volumes in a bookstore, strolling through streets in foreign cities, freedom itself."

"It isn't your nature to give in, sir. That's why everyone respects you. You keep your promises. You have the courage to speak out and aren't afraid to offend either your colleagues or your adversaries. We believe in you, and I for one am willing to follow you anywhere."

"The problem lies elsewhere, Otto. Perhaps I'll set up a new company."

"If you want me, I would be happy to leave with you."

"Unless I settle in the United States, of course. It's a strange feeling to find oneself at a crossroads at my age. I have neither the time nor the right to make a mistake, and I must be careful to choose the correct route. My judgment seems to have deserted me; somehow, I can't think clearly right now. I try to imagine myself collaborating with the new board, but that seems to me impossible. And it also seems absurd to work elsewhere—New York, San Francisco, Bonn, Geneva. I had my next three years planned so clearly, but now I can only make out a wall of heavy fog."

The telephone rang.

A secretary's stiff, formal voice asked Bernt if he could come to see his uncle the next day at eleven. There was no sense in trying to put off the inevitable. As he agreed to the meeting, he thought of how he must try to anticipate the line that the conversation would take, how he must be prepared to face humiliation or else resign. He was going to be obliged to change his tune, to make the transition from boss to employee without losing his dignity. Just like a knight in an ancient Sienese joust, he was to have the opportunity to test his courage against an adversary whose mount wore the colors of destiny. For two days, he had tried to make use of the visionary foresight for which he was celebrated, but his special talent seemed to have deserted him. He felt confusedly that he must forge ahead come what may, press on, without regard for signs of danger, toward a resolution whose shape he could not guess until he drew near to it.

X

As BERNT SLUMPED DOWN IN HIS SOFT LEATHER ARM-chair before the fire Ingrid had lit in the library, Tech, the Labrador, came to lay a sympathetic head on his knee. A Bach cantata that Viveca had just placed on the record player made Bernt think of the Concerto for Clarinet in A Major he and Ulla had listened to together. He had not found the time to call her, and wondered if she were not upset by his silence. If friends had invited her out for the evening, she had probably refused, counting on Bernt to slip away and come to her. Though she was aware that his work kept him from spending enough time with his wife and children, she undoubtedly felt that passion should take precedence over duty and family responsibilities, that a man who spent his day making important decisions should know how to be master of his leisure hours. If Bernt neglected her, she must be-

lieve he did not love her, that she was not indispensable to his happiness. With the clear vision of those in
love, she would conclude that he had simply toyed
with her. She would decide that she had fallen into
bed too hastily; that the man who had showered and
then kissed her good-bye so hurriedly might even
now, his memory clean as a blank sheet of paper, be
on his way to repeat with a different partner what
had been for him merely a bout of sexual gymnastics.
Bernt resolved to send her a basket of flowers with a
tender note the following morning. But he feared that
she would misunderstand and see in his sumptuous
roses an *adieu.*

Viveca appeared with a chess set, followed by Lars
and Axel, and asked Bernt to play. Bernt smiled at his
daughter and told her to sit down and arrange the
board. After she had set up the chess pieces, a proud
expression illuminated Viveca's face and she tossed
back her long curls triumphantly. Poor child! She was
so happy to receive even a tiny portion of his attention. His children were usually asleep when he returned from the bank. He saw them only at Storö,
where he granted them several hours of sailing on
Sundays. Otherwise he barely spoke to them, but
spent the rest of the weekend bent over his papers, or
receiving business acquaintances who had come to
consult with him. At such times, the family was rele-
gated to the back of the house, while Ingrid silently
and discreetly served the food and drinks, then stole
away. He couldn't remember ever having had a conversation with his sons or Viveca about God or love
or death. During a business weekend he had spent at
Windsor, during a brief stay in England, he had been
struck by his industrialist host's behavior with his

children. One by one, he had examined the seashells they had collected in a pail, then he had looked over the butterflies they had captured, and afterward, with the aid of an encyclopedia, he had helped them classify their treasures. Bernt had been amazed at such paternal devotion—a committment that he had never experienced. He himself retreated from his children, kept his distance, limiting personal contact with them to phrases such as: "Have you studied your lessons?" "Are your grades good?" "Wash your hands before sitting down at table." His relations with his children were reduced to a basic computerlike vocabulary, lacking tenderness, intimacy, love.

Bernt taught the boys and Viveca the intricate strategy of the game. They were as delighted to have captured his attention as puppies when caressed by their master. He wondered why he had accorded them so little of his time in the past ten years. He had sacrificed them to the Group, which—irony of ironies—was now going to be removed from his care. If he had paid more attention to his children, would they have been any different? They would have trusted him more, and their confidence would have made communication with them easier and more intimate. School does not resolve all problems, nor does it answer all questions. The professor of natural sciences could show the children anatomical charts and photographs representing a couple making love, but he could not explain to them how to behave when confronting the objects of their passion. They needed their father to help them with the sexual problems involved with love. Would they be able to curb their impulses, govern their inner turmoils? If Bernt had given them more of his time, Lars at sixteen would

come to ask his father at what age he had first slept
with a girl and, when Bernt replied, "At twenty,"
would laugh, saying that he intended to start long before that. Bernt's children would not be so severely
held back as he himself had been in his youth. At
nineteen he had fallen in love with Birgit, a fisherman's pretty daughter in whose company he had discovered a cave at the far end of the beach; by swimming under the rocks covered with seagulls, they had
reached a haven hidden from others, where they had
taken off their bathing suits, and where, after a long,
slow kiss, she had become his with the simplicity of a
summer dawn; death then had seemed far away
indeed. Their secret had been discovered by no one.
He knew that she would never forget those days.
They had swum, made love, gathered seashells, written tender messages in the sand. They had never seen
each other again. They had known that Bernt would
be another person the following summer, that without
having chosen it or wished it they would follow different routes. There had been no chance that their
lives could be led together. Well aware of this, condi-
tioned by the ancient, timeless passivity of women,
resigned to being abandoned, she had held back her
tears. But they had loved each other, despite the fact
that Lars's heir would never be free to marry a fisherman's daughter. His destiny had been to go on
alone—alone in spite of the ballet danced around him
by Birgit, Donatella, Ulla. Ingrid was simply the sister, mother, or cousin whose bed he had the right to
share. He respected her, but she did not have the
power to send him soaring into the magical realm he
had found with Ulla.

Bernt was in bed when Ingrid returned from the

bathroom, looking younger than she did during the day, when her sensible demeanor had the effect of aging her prematurely. Her habitual coldness may have had its origins in the relative indifference of her husband. They were courteous to each other; their relations were based on mutual respect. She had undone her chignon and had donned a new embroidered nightgown with rose satin ribbons at the shoulders. Her French toilet water mingled deliciously with the perfume of the salts she had used in her bath. Was she following the suggestions offered in women's magazines? It was curious that Ingrid should attempt to seduce him; until now he had never neglected her sexually. It was ten o'clock. What was Ulla doing? She had probably waited for him all evening, starting at each sound of the elevator. Had she then retired to her empty bed, disappointed, doubting? Her husband Daniel was due to return on May first, *Valborgsmassoafton* night, that long, dark vigil until the light of day appears, when winter gives way and the dead warriors return to the clearing ringed with birch trees, those trees of death, trees of life. The prehistoric men who had reached this country, rich in forests and fish-filled lakes, after the great spring thaw had given thanks to Lug, whose name signified at once light, whiteness and raven. A black god who reigned over the next world but was also an immaculate seagull, a white dove of peace, he was the spirit of abundance, of resurrection, in whom love and death are mingled. He must telephone Ulla as early as possible the next morning and, if his program were not too overloaded, arrange to meet her at the end of the day, using a late business meeting as his excuse at home.

Carl was lying in wait for him, a spider preparing to lure his victim into his deadly web. He was undoubtedly readying his dossier, turning over the pages with his arthritic hands, having first ordered his wife not to interrupt him for any reason. He was of course going to rake up old disputes, offer false proof that he had gained the confidence of his associates which his nephew had forfeited, using absurd reasons to justify his intentions and strengthen his claims. Bernt shuddered at the idea of being forced to deal with such hypocrisy. The business world had accustomed him to being tested, to walking the razor's edge, ever on guard against a fatal misstep, to controlling whatever violence and anger raged within him, to remaining lucid and calm despite his constitutionally passionate temperament and nervous disposition. Knowing he was lost, he felt a nostalgia for those days when he had ultimately won any battle he had embarked upon. Why had he run afoul of men's small-mindedness, how had he shocked their prejudices? He had always served the Group's best interests. No one else possessed his training, his ability to foresee the future, his faculty for inspiring his staff with the zeal and the faith that move mountains. Carl of all men was the least capable of succeeding him. How ghastly to be forced to hand over the keys to the citadel to that failure, that embittered human being! Bernt had no way of letting the truth be known. The trap had been so well set that there could be no last-minute surprise.

"Darling . . ."

Seated on her bed, Ingrid was looking at him. She obviously had no intention of reading—no book, no magazine lay at hand.

"You haven't said a word all evening. Is something wrong?"

"No, my dear. I'm just tired, that's all."

How could he tell her that he found her perfect but that she lacked that special charm which stirs a man's imagination? He had married her because he knew that she would remain calm and tranquil, that she could be counted on to perform her duties as a trustworthy partner. As it had turned out, she played her role to perfection with the children and with her husband. That was what he had wished, what he had chosen. Women who send chills along a man's spine and make his head spin are not always those to whom he gives his name.

"You haven't told me about your visit to your father."

Bernt drew his sheet up to his chin to indicate that he wanted to sleep.

"Come now," she insisted. "What happened?"

Bernt's voice was elaborately judicious:

"Papa had a nasty cold and was out of sorts. His isolated way of life doesn't agree with him. Or maybe it's his wife who annoys him. He seemed to me stubborn, obstinate, completely dominated by Carl, whom I shall be seeing tomorrow. I may be resigning."

"What will you do, Bernt?"

"I really have no idea. By selling my stock in the Group, I would be breaking all ties with it. I don't wish to damage them or cause them the least difficulty. Outsiders, speculators, would buy my shares, which would mean the end of our business, for they would play a selfish game without any regard for the staff or the family. They would sell to the first comers, pocket the profits, and the best interests of our enterprise be damned. There would no longer be a general policy with an eye to long-term investments. The Group couldn't possibly weather such a course. I can't bring myself to accept such a situation, yet Carl and Nils don't have the means between them to buy me out. So, Ingrid, I'm at a loss, really trapped."

"Couldn't you trust the new management, if there is one, enough to join it?"

"No! It's a question of honor. I'm not about to place myself at the disposition of people trying to do away with me. I may not be able to stop them, but I'm certainly not going to hang around watching them dismantle Grandfather's work."

"Isn't there anyone who can advise you?"

Bernt turned out his bedside lamp.

"I shall wait, watch, determine the lay of the land. All of us Swedes have a bit of the sailor in us. We've learned to read weather signs, we know what it means when the birds migrate. I intend to go on doing the best I can."

Ingrid hesitated, looking at him helplessly.

"Bernt . . ."

He opened his eyes.

"Yes?"

"The prime minister's personal secretary called me last night, because you weren't in your office, to invite us to dinner next month."

"I know. Otto told me."

She continued, without taking her eyes off him:

"I telephoned your father to give you the message. You had already left on the eleven o'clock plane. Bernt, where did you spend the night?"

He turned his back to her. Should he lie? Should he explain that he had needed the solitude of a hotel room? Why bother to answer? It was time that Ingrid learned to ask only those questions whose answers she was capable of understanding.

"Sleep well," he murmured.

XI

BERNT FELT A STRANGE SENSATION: AT THE SAME TIME that he was presiding over the meeting with his executive aides, it seemed to him that he saw his double looking on from the doorway of the board room, wearing a smile on his lips. What had his closest associates heard? Otto, as usual seated on his right, was discreet and trustworthy; he had obviously kept what he knew to himself. Would the others interpret for themselves the rumors that were gliding insidiously as vipers through the business community? So little had sufficed to bring him down. A month earlier, at this same table, supremely sure of himself, Bernt had examined problems that had been submitted to him and had decided their outcomes, had analyzed plans and operating reports, discussed communications sent in by the Rand Corporation, to which he was a subscriber. (To run an investment complex on an international scale required the assistance of futurology technicians, so as to foresee, with a minimum of error, the principal tendencies of the ten years to come.) How far away all that seemed now!

Today, while speaking with his staff, he was at the same time the "other," the Bernt who stood apart at the door, observing the meeting. He could see himself dressed in a white-and-brown tweed jacket and flannel trousers, a yellow shirt bought at Turnbull & Asser in London, a navy-blue club tie with its print of tiny ships' wheels; one of his hands rested on the table, the other mechanically doodled on a block of paper. A matter was being discussed, he was asking for precise details, settling it, reaching a decision whose consequences would be far-reaching. His relatively unlined face and dark brown, slightly curly hair barely revealed that he would soon be celebrating his fortieth birthday. No one could have possibly discerned a shadow of worry or doubt in his attitude. In order to stop the game he was playing with himself, he gave his full attention to the discussion and, although it was like turning a knife in his vitals to do so, went through the motions of polite exchange.

"We must discover how to conquer the top place on the international market. The kind of steel we sell aboard has so far been limited; I believe it important that we extend our markets to naval shipyards. Oil is the vital fluid for highly industrialized countries such as ours. It is dangerous to depend on the good will of the Orient under the aegis of the Soviet Union. One gesture and the tap can be turned off, condemning us to total paralysis. We could be reduced to total impotence—no more tractors, no more factories, no more transportation! Without being able to defend ourselves, lacking the necessary fuel for tanks and planes, we would fall like ripe fruit into the hands of the Russians. The drilling in the North Sea must be speeded up. Insofar as our Group is concerned, negotiations have been entered into with one or our most important shipowners. We must have our own fleet. Sweden is the second most important builder of ships after Japan. This position must be maintained by means of an ever-increasing production. We must maintain optimum flexibility, permitting quick adjustments to new problems based on acquisition of facts; we must ensure price advantages and a technological edge; and we must study the possibility of new mergers to bolster the efficiency of competing companies."

He met Otto's eyes, shining with intelligence, and thought he detected in them a reproach. When he tried to catch his eye a second time, Otto had turned his head away. He was too respectful of the principle of hierarchy to permit himself to judge his superior, but for a moment he had not been able to control a reflex. What right had Bernt to discuss the future objectives of the Group when it was probable that he would soon be ousted and lose all semblance of power within it? If another man were to become chief executive, the attitude of the Group would change. As new director of operations, Carl would create an atmosphere of craft and cunning, favoring those who flattered him, never tolerating an opinion different from his own. He would end by castrating his counselors, who would be forced to choose between giving in to him or resigning.

Bernt pushed back a lock of hair that had fallen over his forehead. Heini Thyssen had telephoned him three days earlier to ask him to lunch in Brussels.

Thyssen had just acquired majority ownership in a steelworks of international proportions, thus becoming the most important figure in modern metallurgy in Europe. Bernt was extremely fond of him, enjoying his esthetic taste, his whimsical imagination that he knew so well how to convert into a formidable weapon when the best interests of his companies so demanded.

Nevertheless, Bernt had declined the invitation to lunch, under pretext of a prior meeting involving difficult negotiations which it was impossible to postpone. Bernt felt as if he were living in a state of limbo, cut off from the company of his peers, the great international barons who, because they were not at the mercy of an electorate empowered to shorten their terms of office, were more important than heads of state.

Bernt's double watched him closely as he declared that Sweden was a country in which individual effort was the least profitable, as could be attested to by the innumerable Swedish accounts flourishing in Swiss banks; that the march of industrial efficiency was in danger of slowing down due to tax hikes outweighing wage gains and an expanded welfare system whose payments were the highest in the world; that a worldwide recession was disrupting vital export markets.

"Percy Mellon has informed me that his family intends to sell about two million shares of the Aluminum Company of America. He asked if we wished to buy. Before the next board meeting, I would like to have your opinion."

Who could have guessed that this executive who spoke in such a calm, steady voice had left his home in the small hours of the morning, before breakfast?

Ingrid had been asleep, or had pretended to sleep. After dressing in the bathroom, Bernt had quietly descended the staircase and entered his car.

The Mercedes had rolled along avenues bordered with trees and houses surrounded by gardens, then proceeded to boulevards where the street lights reflected the silhouettes of barges laden with sand, cement, wood, sailing down the estuary. Aloft, seagulls had floated in from the islands in small squadrons, carried along gently by the wind.

Five eighteen-floor towers dominated the buildings, whose height decreased as the distance increased from the center of Stockholm, until at the edge of the woods they became small individual houses. Bernt had caught sight of Ulla's skyscraper, the shops and the ultramodern offices of the commercial and sociocultural center, just as dawn had been lazily appearing over the rooftops.

She had opened the door, half-asleep, a bathrobe thrown over her shoulders. He had seized her in his arms and carried her to the bed. How had he been able to live through an entire day without her? Daniel would be back in three days. Bernt preferred not to think of him installed in that room, sleeping in the adjoining twin bed.

He felt as though he were jumping from the top of a cliff into the sea. Nothingness, the void, must resemble this plunge into the liquescent heart of what was after all nothing more than a vital impulse, a race towards life, inexhaustible energy. When his parents had made love, this same impulse had shot forth two million spermatozoa storming at the gates of life. One alone, Bernt, had won the race, while the others vanished forever.

Was he the son of the young couple Nils and Lena,
or the child of the old pirate? The doubt opened up a
wound that death alone could heal. He felt dazed, as
though stunned by a long fall. War? Like his fellow
citizens, he had never waged it. Illness? He had never
been sick. Fatigue? Unknown to him. But how could
he surmount this growing canker, this nausea, this las-
situde, this urge toward death? He had freed himself
from Lars's iron hand by means of a personal success
to which he had consecrated all his adult energies. He
had triumphed in a milieu in which the weak cannot
survive. His energy was linked to his migratory instinct. Bernt had responded intellectually and spiritu-
ally to the countries he had visited; travel had
stimulated his mental faculties; his aim had been to
meet, to communicate, to give and to take, to widen
his horizons.

He thought of the *silvertarnän* whose annual mi-
gration covers thirty thousand kilometers. There is always a further destination such birds must reach, in
defiance of death, so as to be delivered from anguish.
They cross mountain ridges and forests, wastelands
and prairie, lakes bordered with birch trees reflecting
the image of a glacier, the tundra and the desert;
they risk being crushed against the steep faces of the
Himalayas, allow themselves to be carried away to
the blue-green icebergs of the Antarctic, to die of exhaustion in the sands of Arabia. These wanderers are
haunted by the desire to push on ever further in their
search for happiness—or for a mirage. They must continue their voyage out of all reason, keep flying in a
straight line seven thousand meters above the earth,
rhythmically beating their wings, propelling themselves ever forward, while the redbreast and the tit

never leave their native woods. The vanquished fall along the way, while the others continue on, unconcerned about the fate of their weaker companions. They reach the end of their journey only to retrace their steps, once more pushing themselves to the limits of their endurance before returning to the elm and the birch, the oak and the fir, the streams and the lakes of Sweden.

Ulla, her hair tumbled about her shoulders, had held an exhausted Bernt in her arms and comforted him as tenderly as a mother reassuring a hurt child. Little by little he had relaxed; nothing else but Ulla and love existed for him.

But then, a second time, he had had to tear himself away, to dress in haste and promise to return the same evening, to jump into his car, try to clear his head for the coming meeting.

"The meeting is over!"

Otto followed Bernt into his office.

"Your report was interesting, sir. You are right about the need to look for new outlets. The partnership with Christer Linders will expand our field of activity."

He hesitated.

"Do you think that if the change in administration about which you spoke to me yesterday should take place, your Uncle Carl would endorse such a point of view?"

"We shall see. I'm going to meet with him this morning at eleven."

Bernt pushed the button on his interphone.

"Margret, I'm leaving and will be back in an hour or so."

Otto regarded him with a puzzled expression.

"He's not coming here?"

Bernt put an arm around Otto's shoulder.

"If it pleases him, why should it bother me to be driven to his office? Prepare the Volvo report for me. I need to know if Volvo might be able to compete adequately on the world market with BMW."

When the door had closed behind Otto, Bernt sat down at his desk, his elbows on the mahogany table, his chin on his hands. The passionate avidity that had devoured him was gone, his thirst for life vanished. His need to become invincible, to accumulate, to grow no longer obsessed him; the motor that fed his energy had stopped. He wanted only to give up, to renounce, to withdraw. His appetite for building an empire and for becoming the foremost industrial titan, his projects for the maximum expansion of the Group, his relationship with political leaders, with international industrialists, with famous journalists, with men of power and influence, his delight in innovations—which lay at the root of his activities—all that was going to be brought into question. He was a born leader and knew how to steer his ship; his decisions were determined not by plodding ratiocination but by intuition and courage. What would he now decide—to give in, to wait, to bow his head calmly until the storm had passed? Would he be forced in the name of democratic principles to resign, letting it be known that a majority had voted for it? If only the Socialist government, which had been in power for forty years, had nationalized the corporations! But ninety-five percent of all commerce, banking, and industry had remained in the private sector. Social leveling had been accomplished by taxation. If Bernt's fate had depended on the prime minister, the latter would never have thought of questioning his management of the investment complex. The charts spoke for themselves—the headway made by the Group was spectacular! But of what use was all that to Bernt now? Just as a cabinet minister was never chosen for his competence but rather on the basis of his personal ties with the man in power, so four decades of resentment were transferred with interest onto the shoulders of the heir to the great Lars's empire.

Would Carl keep him waiting? The doorman recognized him and bowed. Bernt had not returned to the headquarters of the prefabricated-housing company of which his uncle was president since the inauguration of the new installation eight years earlier.

The secretary asked him to accompany her. From behind the huge desk which served him as a rampart, Carl asked Bernt to take a seat. Balding, weasel-faced, his uncle was stiffly clad in a banal white shirt, a somberly dark tie, and a solemn blue tweed suit, which conspired to give him the look of a dour prosecuting attorney.

"Thank you for taking the trouble to come to my office," he said rapidly, as though hurrying through an unpleasant duty.

Bernt smiled.

"I wanted to see you too. We could have lunched together."

Carl replied stiffly: "I can understand that the importance of work makes it difficult for you to take a meal with members of your family who are not of immediate usefulness to you. You usually place the interests of the Group above all else. We are grateful, but you do have a tendency to make no distinction between your own person and our companies."

Bernt remained silent, concentrating his attention on his interlocutor. If only he had practised the technique of Buddhist meditation, then his mind would have become empty and clear, and he would have been able to forget his pain.

"Are you listening to me?" Carl almost shouted. "My brother spoke to me about your visit to him. I know that you are now aware of our agreement."

"What agreement?"

"You know perfectly well! Our enterprise has not done as brilliantly as you would have everyone believe. You are dangerous because you are too arrogant, too self-confident. Your stupendous conceit warps your judgment."

A person, an object, a system contains within itself the germ of its own destruction. At what exact moment had Bernt crossed the threshold of insecurity? That nasal, high-pitched voice had perhaps finished him off.

"Nils and I, as principal shareholders, have no reason to simply sit by and allow you to act as you see fit. You have never taken our suggestions into consideration, but on the contrary have behaved as though we did not exist. You make us run useless risks, for example by trying to invest in that oil-tanker consortium. That is not our line. We would be too diversified."

Bernt leaned on the desk.

"The future must be thought of, Uncle Carl. You wish to replace me. Very well. But then you must expect a downswing in your turnover and profits. We are at a point where it is essential that we make the proper choices. Remember the difficulties we had with that mineral that was too loaded with phosphorus, and the problems we had about exportation?"

Carl's mouth, thin and sharp as a blade, stretched in a slight grimace.

"You've never felt the need of consulting me about anything before! When did you ever telephone to ask for my advice? I imagine that you even found it disagreeable to be forced to see me."

"Please, Uncle Carl! We can't afford to make a mistake; we must be farsighted in order to keep our competitive edge. Our margin for self-financing is becoming increasingly narrow. The national tax on our profits has risen to forty percent, plus twenty percent for the townships. I've thought about the problem for two years and have come up with a plan. Do you wish to hear it?"

A flash of irony illuminated Carl's reptilian eyes.

"You are full of dedication and devotion, my dear Bernt, but you have one defect. Once you have established a plan, you believe that you hold the secret of innate scientific truth. You have a tendency to take the rest of the world for idiots. Why have you come to see me? Why are you so amiable, when heretofore you have never given a damn for my opinion? I won't even speak of your cousins, to whom you have paid no attention whatever. My father made you president of the Group in a moment of aberration due to his age. You were convinced that your privileged position would last your lifetime. An error, my dear Bernt! A profound error."

"What do you have against me, Uncle Carl?"

Carl raised a bony, blue-veined white hand to silence him.

"Let's not become personal, please. Nils and I discussed the situation and arrived at the conclusion that you would make an excellent general manager."

"I?" Bernt asked, unable to control a start of surprise.

"You will no longer make decisions about the Group's investments on your own. You will have to learn to consult us, my dear nephew, beforehand. That is natural and normal—we are your elders."

Of what use would it be to tell his uncle that he, Carl, unlike himself, did not personally know the chief executives of the great international companies, and that once Bernt was reduced in rank and thereby discredited their trust would be lost?

"You are not an oracle, my boy," Carl continued. "How can you predict what will happen in the months to come? Perhaps my brother will return to Stockholm. Did he mention such a possibility to you? No! Although I am not familiar with marketing, merchandising, and so on, I am better informed than you are."

"But Father has lost the habit of dealing with business affairs. The only thing he's done all these years is take care of his forests."

(For thirty-eight years, Bernt had called Nils "Father," and now he did not know how to refer to him.)

"Whatever you may think, my boy, Nils is not finished; I am happy that I was able to convince him to return to his place among us."

Bernt's larynx tightened; he painfully cleared his throat.

"Well, Uncle, I see no reason why we cannot establish a triumvirate."

The thin lips stretched into a sarcastic smile.

"I believed you to be intelligent. You don't seem to

understand that you have set our teeth on edge for years with your conceit, your insistence upon ruling the Group as chief executive with full powers and alone, as though you had received a mandate from heaven. To each his turn! Your shares are outnumbered by those of my children, Nils, and myself combined. You hold a minority vote, and therefore must give in. If you prefer to continue to work with us, and we all devoutly hope you will, you will have the title of General Manager, which is an honorable enough position for someone your age. Your rise was too rapid. We shall announce this decision at the next meeting, on May tenth. Please don't argue; don't waste your time or mine. Our decision is irrevocable."

"But I own twenty thousand shares!"

"Who will buy them? You know as well as I that they are worthless if you are not a majority shareholder."

"Splendid! You will become president on May tenth. What a triumph! What a revenge! To succeed to your father's place after all these years—at your age!"

Bernt was panting as though he had just run a hundred-meter race.

"What a master stroke! I congratulate you! We must now think of the future of the Group. I had anticipated an agreement with Christer Linders. I'll send you the documents concerning that transaction."

Carl opened a drawer and took out a file folder.

"You seem to ignore the existence of photocopy machines, my boy. I have the same documents as you. Thanks for your advice!"

Bernt rose. He was seized by a deadly chill.

"Good-bye, Uncle Carl. I'm sorry that you are so full of resentment."

Carl remained seated, the victorious spider squatting triumphantly in the center of his web.

As Bernt went toward the elevator his heart beat violently, his temples throbbed, his body felt white-hot. Outdoors, the icy air came as a shock to him. He got into the car without a word and Werner quietly closed the door; the chauffeur understood his need for silence.

What Bernt faced was inevitable. He could put off the moment of his downfall, but he could not escape it any more than the bull in the arena can elude the *banderillas* and the sword. The animal fights on alone, not by instinct, since he knows what awaits him, but out of stubborn principle, to the sound of trumpets saluting his courage, his pride. He charges, head lowered, towards those who torture him, dances a final ballet with the matador, and at last, deciding to abandon the combat, allows his adversary to administer the coup de grâce.

Stockholm's palaces, its ancient churches and old private houses were surrounded by glass, concrete, and steel. Watching the pedestrians waiting for the lights to change, it was difficult to distinguish the executive from the worker, the boy from the girl; all wore warm coats muffled up around their necks and caps that covered their ears. Sweden was second after the United States in having the highest mean annual income, the longest lifespan; its citizens enjoyed one television set for every four persons, one car for every three, one telephone for every two, the best system of social insurance. Strikes, poverty, unemployment, slums had been conquered; gone were those days of famine which at the beginning of the century had caused one Swede out of ten to emigrate.

The wide, silent avenues, the large exterior boulevards, the green, well-cared-for parks, the traffic pattern so conceived that each car could roll along in its own line without stopping, explained the fact that Sweden had such a low number of automobile accidents. But how about the other calamities that might befall a man? Those which throw him to the ground when he has not deserved it; those which tear from him the attributes of his power without which he does not know how to live! How can a man muster the strength to smile and go on as if nothing had happened when he has been stripped of his prerogatives? How could he have foreseen that the foundations of his power would be undermined by his uncle's bitterness—and with his father's blessing?

The Mercedes came to a stop before the Group's headquarters. Every morning when he arrived, Bernt would drink in the lines of that edifice, with its strange enduring beauty, which seemed to affirm his immortality. The sight of that pure cube of glass and aluminum towering at the edge of the vast conglomeration of modern buildings that housed the home offices of Stockholm's great industrial, banking, aviation, and commercial houses—the Stockholm of the future—always awoke in him a sensation of inner music, as if he were hearing the first measures of a symphony; it was the same impression he had when, in autumn, the birch trees shimmered in their dress of gold, or when he saw barges laden with logs to the water line entering the arms of the Baltic that flowed into Lake Mälar.

Today that serene harmony was missing; in its

place there remained only an overwhelming, echoing silence. He opened the car door and stepped onto the sidewalk before Werner had time to react.

"Thanks. I'll be down in half an hour."

He asked Margret to give him a résumé of the morning's calls, then telephoned Ingrid, who answered him in monosyllables. Undoubtedly he had annoyed her. But he had no excuses or explanations to give her; there were more urgent things for him to attend to.

"Are the children all right? I have to be away for two days on a very important trip. Don't worry."

She remained silent. Something was evidently troubling her. Bernt pitied her, but he had no choice.

"Will you be stopping at the house to get what you need?"

He adopted the professional tone of voice that never failed to impress his wife.

"I won't have time. I'll buy a shirt and handkerchiefs at the airport. Take good care of the children. Give them my love. A good-bye kiss, my dear."

His voice failed him and he hung up. Poor girl! She wasn't accustomed to such offhand treatment. Bernt leafed through his calendar. He was to see the prime minister at six o'clock. Margret rang the number for him and put him through to the personal secretary.

"Madame Ekelöf? Something's come up; I won't be able to meet with the prime minister this afternoon. Would you put me through to him? Perhaps he can tell me on the phone what he had in mind."

If old Lars had allowed him to follow his natural inclinations, Bernt would have liked to be a politician. In the present mixed regime, the old capitalist-socialist antagonism was passé; time-honored enemies had become partners. In today's policy of coexistence, in which confidence—rather than suspicion—and cooperation between the two great parties was the rule, the aim was efficiency, not the squandering of precious energy in fratricidal struggles that could only weaken the country's economic relations abroad. The citizens' interests came first and not the personal ambitions of individuals.

The young, cheerful voice of the prime minister came over the wire.

"What's the trouble, Bernt?"

"A nasty problem. I have to concentrate on how to deal with it, so I'm clearing out for two days to think things over. Will you forgive me if I don't make it today?"

"Of course."

"You wanted to talk to me about something specific?"

"I meant to talk to you about striking a balance, Bernt. Human beings are like countries—some are more advanced than others. A hundred and fifty years ago in this country, we realized that going to war held up a nation's progress. We learned how to avoid general strikes—which are almost as damaging as war—by prior agreement between employers and employees. Instead of drawing the moral *after* a catastrophe we like to avoid it by thinking *ahead* to its possible effects."

"Why are you telling me this?"

"A human being is like society," the prime minister went on. "My job is to run this country, to foresee the changes it will go through. I've become a doctor in spite of myself. I make a practice of analyzing symptoms and uncovering trouble while there's time to do something about it. My job consists in defusing bombs before they go off. With people as well as with countries, I'm a good diagnostician. I know how to pick up the signs of catastrophes before they happen. To answer your question more directly, if you had come to see me I would have talked to you about yourself, Bernt. Don't do anything stupid. An adult's worth is measured by the way he reacts to adversity."

A silence ensued. So the prime minister had heard. How long ago? What did it matter! The die had been cast. All that remained was to find a way to leave the table as gracefully as possible.

"What are you going to do, Bernt?"

Otto had asked the same question. How was he to answer? Should he say, "I'm going to take a rest," or, "I haven't the slightest idea"?

"I don't know. I'm going to take forty-eight hours to think it over."

The prime minister spoke more emphatically, his voice even warmer than before.

"I myself am never satisfied, Bernt. Our comfortable society has a million flaws, the first and foremost being the scandalous effect it has on the developing countries. Two-thirds of the planet are miserable, while we in the West enjoy considerable luxury. That's one of the major problems I think about—how to jolt the rich out of their selfish apathy and give those who are just emerging from the Bronze Age a means of living decently! No matter what worries I have, Bernt, I face up to them. Sometimes when my own friends attack me, or when I hear about an act of disloyalty on the part of a colleague, I'm sad indeed. Often I'm discouraged, but still I go on fighting. The man who fights back, Bernt, always wins in the end. You must never give up! Now I realize that you're going through a difficult period, even a painful one. No matter what you decide to do, remember that I consider you one of my advisors. I count on you, I need you."

When the prime minister had hung up, Bernt pressed the button on the intercom. "Margaret, will you ask Otto to come in?"

The young man entered a moment later and Bernt waved him to a chair.

"What I anticipated has happened, Otto. At the next meeting, on May tenth, my uncle Carl will take my place. I want you to stay on here. You're the most important man on my staff. What is happening here is only a . . . change . . . of . . . personnel. The business itself is healthy and prosperous; we are constantly expanding. No one, after all, is indispensable."

"But . . ."

Bernt assumed a brusque manner.

"My uncle and I disagree on a fundamental question. I wish to engage the Group in a policy of fuel independence, in North Sea drilling and supertankers. The diversification of our enterprises makes it possible for us to engage in investment on a vast scale. My father and uncle, who are the majority stockholders, think otherwise. I bow to their wishes. It's all due to the fact that there's a difference in generations, a real generation gap. We don't look at the future from the same angle."

As he spoke, Otto's eyes never left his face. An affection which, owing to modesty or reticence, he failed to express openly, showed clearly in his shocked expression. He listened carefully, not missing a word or an intonation; Bernt knew that Otto would fight to see that whatever instructions were given him were carried out.

"I'll be gone for two days. I need quiet. I'm going to fly to Kiruna, to my shooting lodge in the forest. Only you will know where to find me. Here's the telephone number. I prefer that you don't use it."

"What about the prime minister?"

"I called him; everything's in order. I'm leaving you the keys to my safe. My personal papers are in it."

Otto made a gesture of protest. Bernt went on.

"Accidents can happen. I know that I can depend on you. If anything should happen to me, I expect you to take care not only of any problems affecting my wife and children, but also my current business affairs. You'll find a signed document to that effect among my papers. I have no illusions about how much trust I can place in my family, now that they have shown me what I can expect from them."

He got to his feet. "So long, Otto."

The tall silhouette withdrew, a world of unspoken questions still registering on his astonished face. Alone once more, Bernt dialled Ulla's number. It had not occurred to him that she might be out. He was annoyed when she did not reply, then took out his wallet. The business card that she had given him at their first meeting bore the number of Christer Linders's office. He had forgotten that she worked with her father. The secretary answered and passed him through to Ulla, who sounded surprised.

He explained that it was impossible for him to join her that evening. He had decided to take some time off to rest. Could she get out of her obligations for two days and go with him to Kiruna? If she agreed, he would show her the forest.

"I need to get away to a place where it's quiet. Come with me. You'll be back by noon on May first. Could you work that out?"

He was unprepared for her reaction. She had been so ardent only hours before, and now he divined in her an astonishing reserve. She replied that her father was waiting for her to edit a report; she had not yet finished and needed two or three hours to do so; her father would mind terribly if she disappointed him; couldn't he put off his trip?

How could she weigh a journey with him against her mundane routine? Impatiently, Bernt interrupted her:

"Do you think it was easy for me to get free? I had an appointment with the prime minister; I canceled it. Find a way, Ulla."

She remained on the defensive. "What about your family?"

"I told my wife that I was leaving. I don't have to account to anyone for what I do. You should never justify your actions. Don't make me lose precious time, Ulla. What's your decision?"

"What about my things?"

"I'll buy you whatever extras you need. Just bring a pair of trousers, two sweaters, warm boots, a sheepskin jacket. Hurry up. You have two hours."

She burst out laughing. She could see why he was such a success—he never lost sight of his objective.

But how could she know that this time Bernt no longer had his objective in sight? He felt as though he were groping in a dark, night-enshrouded place where there were neither perspective nor direction to guide him. Death must resemble that flat, uniform territory veiled in mists, where shadows lurked. A purgatory without trees or rivers, without flowers or dwelling places, where a murky dawn obscured the shape of things.

"Ulla, make up your mind. Are you coming with me?"

She was silent.

"Ulla! Are you letting me down?"

Still she hesitated. Couldn't he put himself in her place? She was dependent on her father, to whom she would be obliged to make excuses. She wasn't only Linders's daughter, but his right hand as well. How could she cancel two days of appointments, obligations, meetings? In the business world, a woman must be ten times more punctual, more precise, more well-organized than a man; every eye was watching her, waiting for her first misstep. If the shipbuilder were to discover that she was neglecting her professional responsibilities to go away with a man, even if he learned that the man was Bernt, he would fire her. He was actually capable of telling her husband what she had done.

"Papa can be terrifying!" she cried. "I'd love to come with you, but I need time to think it over." She lowered her voice: "Did I shut my door to you this morning?"

Bernt made an effort to control his voice. He was beside himself, outraged. He had broken his ties with Stockholm, with his family, with the prime minister, with his colleagues. The only presence in all the world that he wanted was Ulla's. Was it possible that she might fail him?

"My plane takes off at three. I'll wait till the last

minute. If you don't make it, Ulla, then this is good-
bye. Thank you for everything."

Beyond the bay, the city vibrated under the cloud-
filtered sunlight. Above its rooftops, birds floated, carried along on the wind's currents, falling like stones,
then rising with the beat of a wing to rejoin the sky.
A *silvertarnän* flew close to the window before which
Bernt sat immobile, opened its violet beak in an inau-
dible cry, then plunged headlong into the void.

XII

SNOW SOFTENED THE OUTLINES OF THE FIR TREES THAT
surrounded the park. Only a man as iron-willed as old
Lars could have succeeded in transforming the clearing into a garden. If his wishes had been carried out,
rose beds and sweet peas, a border of fuchsias, and
graveled walks edged with box would have been
added. The landscape gardener he had brought from
Stockholm had made the best he could of the space
left in the midst of the centuries-old trees by earlier
settlers. This leafy Trianon had been created by the
offspring of a family of woodcutters who had succeeded in escaping from his social class. After mounting the social hierarchy, he had been motivated by
a sharp urge to have his revenge on those who had
humiliated him along the way. He considered this unusual house to be a symbol of his success. As a
student, looking at his parents' struggles—his mother

raising as best she could six children in three rooms, their limited education (there had not been one book in that house), Lars had had the impression of having come an infinite distance, of having been literally wrenched out of his natural orbit. During his school vacations, he had helped his father split wood. How he had regretted not being able to talk to him about poetry, books, the theories he found so enthralling! He had long been aware of his isolation among his own people. He had been close to his eldest brother Hans, who was a cod fisherman, and had counseled his sister Dagmar on her choice of suitors. But their relations had stopped short as though blocked by an invisible threshold. They avoided questions that would have challenged their inner comfort; they neglected opportunities that might have transformed their lives. Routine had been all-important. One July evening, when Lars had been absorbed in a treatise on financial mathematics, his mother had looked on in astonishment.

"Why do you tire yourself so, my son? Your father would prefer that you help him repair his axe. Aren't you happy with us? Why must you go to the city?"

He had put an arm around her.

"In the fall, you've seen the cranes flying in formation, Mother. One bird leads and the others follow, their wings flapping furiously as they fly ever faster, ever higher. I too feel an urge to fly away, to be free. Do you know what the word 'Viking' means? 'He who embarks for distant places.' They weren't content to stay on their own shore but were impelled to explore the world, to sail the Black Sea and the Caspian, arrive at Byzantium, and trade with the peoples of Asia. I feel a kinship with them. I can't bear to think that I might die without ever having walked the streets of New York! In Vancouver I want to see the forests denser than ours growing down to the shores of the Pacific, I want to hear the icy night wind blowing over Peking, to see the pink reflections of the Libyan mountains in the Nile, to meditate by the lily pond at the pagoda in Kyoto, to be silent in awe before Kishi!"

"What is Kishi, my son?"

"An island in the middle of Lake Onega, in Russia, where two centuries ago a woodworker carved a wonderful city, cupolas in the shape of bulbs covered with scales as round as those of carps, churches crowned with helmets, windmills whose wings are as light as dreams." Lars spoke gently. "Do you understand why I've worked so hard, Mama? The scholarships I've won have helped me go on with my education. I don't want to be a prisoner! Some creatures never leave their nests. Others know how to exceed the limits of endurance, to risk death for the pleasure of surpassing themselves."

His mother had stroked her son's hair but had not been able to grasp what he wished to express.

"The important thing is to rattle one's chains! I keep my eyes fixed on the road. I'm not afraid of death—but laugh at it. To compete against my own self gives me the illusion that I understand eternity. I think that must be what birds feel as they fly near to the sun."

Lars's mother, ill-at-ease when the conversation turned to unfamiliar subjects, had hesitantly told him a legend she had heard from her grandmother: On one side of a river, near a ford, were a herd of white reindeer. On the other shore brown reindeer grazed.

Each time that a white reindeer brayed in a certain way, a brown reindeer would leave its companions and cross the rocky shallows. As soon as it reached the other side, it lost its color and became immaculately white. On the other hand, whenever a brown reindeer uttered that particular cry, a white animal would cross the river to join it, and at that moment it would take on a chestnut tint. This is how mankind crosses the frontier which separates the land of the dead from that of the living, explained Lars's mother. The two are superimposed, one on the other, and a network of intermediaries permits the invisible to communicate with the material world.

Lars, who had told this story to Bernt, had believed it to be a myth dating back to the builders of megaliths, those Hyperboreans who had worshipped the sun goddess. When business had allowed the old man and his grandson some respite, they would spend many hours devoted to conversations about subjects far removed from the world of industry. Bernt had appreciated Lars's scholarship, which he had acquired without detriment to the richness of his imagination or to the originality of his viewpoint. Despite the difference in their ages, the boy had seemed to be his only friend. The old pirate had hated society, limiting himself to professional contacts, which he had carried on without sentimentality—he had been renowned for his hardheadedness. If Lars were at his side there in the lodge, what advice would he give him? The snow wove its woolen threads against the window panes; a wood fire kept Bernt company. The silence restored to him that subtle sense that allows us to delve deep into the heart of the matter that concerns us most, to understand the mechanics of our own soul. In what measure must one accept the impossible?

If he were to resign, it would be tantamount to acknowledging an error he had not committed. If he were to fight Carl and Nils, it would delight the Group's rivals, confuse those who had confidence in it, destroy what he had built up with his own hands. As Bernt threw a log onto the embers, they flared up in a blue flame. The hours ticked by. Bernt experienced a feeling of great remoteness as the wind's wails rose like the cries of lost souls pursued by ancient trolls.

He had waited at the airport until the last second. Sitting with an overnight case between his knees, he had watched for Ulla to appear. He imagined her coming toward him, emerging from the crowd, a goddess by Botticelli, her green eyes growing tender at the sight of him.

An insistent voice coming over the public address system had jolted him back to reality. His plane was about to take off. Bernt had cast a final look at the glass entrance doors. He had given her two hours to make up a plausible story for Christer Linders, to finish her report, run home and change, jump into a taxi and reach the airport. It was not surprising that she had not been able to make it.

He passed through the turnstile, entered the waiting room, showed his boarding pass, and crossed the tarmac to the foot of the gangway. Why had he believed that Ulla would drop everything and come with him? Somehow, he had never doubted that she would not. His confidence in his own star had been worth any number of victories; but now his self-assurance had suffered a devastating blow. Had his luck

turned against him? That morning she had taken him
in her arms and given herself to him as docile as the
sea receiving the prow of a ship; he had believed that
her mind belonged to him as well. Now it appeared
that she could not escape the domination of her father. Did this unexpected defeat presage others?

Bernt had drawn the curtains against the wind's
blasts, which were causing the branches to break and
the treetops to bend, raising a cacophony of hostile
sounds. Out there Odin in his speeding chariot was
searching out his victim.

At Storö, when Bernt had been a child, he had
been obliged to go to bed first, because he had been
the youngest. He would run up the stairs and hurry to
slam the door of his room, with its walls and floor of
blond wood in which, from the safety of his bed, he
would count the knots. How long would the window
resist the pressure of the gale? He had dreamed that
his mother was leaning over his bed to tuck him in.
One day he had discovered in one of his grandmother's drawers a box containing old photographs.
There were snapshots of a family picnic at the house
in Stockholm, of Lena in the shade of the copper
beeches, of Lars with his hawk's profile, of Lena on a
beach, wearing a swim suit and laughing as she dried
herself with a Turkish towel. Her vitality had seemed
to spill over out of the snapshot; she resembled a
dryad, closer to nature than to the sophistication of
the city. There had been many of the black-and-white
snapshots. In the later pictures, Lena's spontaneity
had left her, her glance had been filled with uneasiness. Had those been the days when she had joined
Lars in the lodge at Kiruna? The furnishings had not
changed since those days. In the room with Bernt

were the same English chairs and tables, velvet hangings, trophies—all of it just as it had been then, intact as was the collection of guns displayed against its panel of Cordova leather. Some of the weapons dated from the time of Charles XII and Gustave Wasa. Lars's pair of Purdeys reposed on their rack. He had used the two guns alternatively, for the reindeer or for the wolves whose ivory-fanged heads adorned the stairwell.

Bernt ran his fingers over the carved stocks, the damascened silver barrels. His mother had lived in this house; it seemed to him that he could almost touch her. Had she cooked the meals while Lars worked? Had they taken walks together in the woods? Had they stretched out side by side on the white bearskins?

Bernt awoke as dawn was breaking. He had fallen asleep on the sofa. A few fragments of wood remained in the fireplace. His eyes still heavy with sleep, he went to the kitchen and made himself some breakfast. The evening before, he had been like a sleepwalker, haunted by strange, inexplicable dreams and impressions. In his nightmare-haunted sleep, Ulla-Lena, now one woman, had called out to him for help. Green waters, clifflike waves, had come crashing down over her head; she had screamed as the seas crushed her. The ancient gods seemed to be demanding expiation. If the old pirate had died at the height of his career, enormously wealthy and covered with honors, his grandson was being sacrificed to appease the anger of those gods, an anger evidently not placated by the death of another victim—Lena.

Bernt felt as though he were the plaything of an instinct stronger than his will, of an obscure racial memory, a puppet obeying the same million-year old compulsion as those birds that fly at fixed intervals toward determined regions. His existence seemed to him a story without beginning or end, a fragment from which the introduction and conclusion were missing. He saw himself as a tributary flowing down out of the generations which had gone before him, from the lemur that had dwelt in trees seventy million years before to the primate feeding on fruits and leaves fifty million years later, and then to the upright carnivore who, three and a half million years before our own time, had known how to polish flint. Under the veneer of modern civilization, there remained unchanged the same terror of the night, the same prehistoric fears, the same dread lest the sun forget to return to the land of shadows, the same anguish regarding the inevitability of age and death.

His birth had had its origins in tragedy and his future seemed to him precarious and uncertain. He had taken refuge in the forest lodge, to which his mother had come stealthily for secret assignations, as instinctively as salmon swim upstream to beach themselves among the reeds. He was finally alone in the most absolute sense—Ingrid and his children, Carl, Nils, and even Ulla had become merely distant strangers.

Except for Otto, who would surely resign, his executive aides would adapt themselves quickly to the new formula. Three or four months hence they would have forgotten him. His name would be mentioned perhaps on the occasion of some anniversary, the annual party for the Group's executives and employees, or at Christmas. There would remain a handful of photographs of him, which Ingrid would never find time to paste in the family album. One day Viveca or

Axel would find it amusing to spread them on the carpet and rediscover their father's face.

Bernt forced himself to take a chicken wing from the refrigerator, which he ate standing up. The second night had just fallen. It was quiet; he imagined he heard the light crunch of a fox's feet on the snow's surface. Before his eyes there appeared an image of his own corpse drifting, its bones white as seashells, trailing shreds of desiccated flesh. His skeleton, held together by tendons, slowly came apart; he saw a tibia, individual vertebrae, his skull, a fibula, scattered, dissolving into dust.

In an effort to calm his nerves, he went upstairs and ran a scalding hot bath. His body seemed to him a ridiculous, paltry thing. What good had it done him to seek out the shades of Lena and Lars? The most painful part of all was that he had loved the man who had formed him, who had taught him everything he knew. And now he was suffering the tortures of the damned because of Lars's duplicity. Bernt could no longer believe in him; the marvelous stone statue had been revealed as no more than a plaster cast.

Bernt went to bed without turning on his lamp. It is said that Fate reserves special tests for those she loves. Would he be given the strength to face them? For the moment, he felt himself emptied, stripped of reactions, exhausted. He dozed, to waken a few hours later at the sound of a loud report, then a thundering explosion. It was the thaw, rending the iron yoke which for so many long months had gripped the torrents and the lakes. The sound foreshadowed the end of the snows, the return of life. The flowers were holding themselves in readiness to burst through their dissolving blanket. It was the moment in which light delivers men from fear, when the troll-haunted darkness is no more!

Bernt dressed and put on his fur-lined raincoat. In the garage stood Lars's Bentley, unchanged from the days when he and Lena had used it, with its pearl-gray upholstery, the cornet of cut glass in which she had stuck a Christmas rose. Its tires left a light track on the snow-covered road. Bernt drove past a crossroads where several roads converged in the shape of a star, and parked under a fir tree. As he advanced at a brisk pace in the direction of the torrent, his boots traced their calligraphy in the snow. The icy air cut his face. What impulse had seized him to go out in the middle of the night to greet the arrival of spring? He leaned against a tree trunk, panting. An embankment, rendered almost phosphorescent by the moonlight, overhung the river that bristled with a crust already deeply gashed by the thaw, fissured as mud when it dries in the desert. The gurgling, bubble-streaked current pressed against its transparent, fragile covering. In the icy prism the captive rainbow's seven colors had been effaced, become as invisible as leaves hidden in the trunks of dead trees. A branch snapped on the other side of the torrent. Bernt saw a man wearing a parka, ski pants, and a woolen cap, staring in fascination at the water coursing free from its icy bounds.

"Fiskar ni laxforeller så här dags?"

The stranger startled, obviously not understanding. Realizing that he was a foreigner, Bernt rephrased his question in English, asking his nationality.

"I am French."

"What I first asked was whether you were fishing for trout at this hour."

The young man made a megaphone of his hands and shouted:

"I can't hear you very well."

"Come and join me then!"

The stream was too wide to be jumped in one bound. The young man tested the edge with his foot and, when it bore his weight, leaped from block to block on a ford made of ice, until he arrived at the other side. Bernt held out a hand to help him up the last few feet of the embankment.

"It isn't exactly a warm night. Would you like to continue our conversation in my car?"

Why should he not offer hospitality to this companion sent by the gods? In extending his invitations to the young stranger, Bernt acknowledged an intervention, perhaps a command, come from powers beyond his sphere.

XIII

HE WAS ASTONISHED TO FIND HIMSELF WISHING HE could unburden his mind and heart to this Frenchman who knew how to listen, and whose hazel eyes shone with such intelligence and soothing calm. His guest reclined in an armchair, his legs comfortably stretched out on a vast, square footstool, having come into his house as a neighbor might, bringing comfort in a difficult time. Bernt's high position and enormous prestige had put a distance between him and the friends of his university days. He had companions, but they were merely casual acquaintances from among his peers, international financiers with whom he was linked by a community of interests. The slightest variation in the index of the prices of raw materials commanded the attention of such men—they could translate it into a Niagara of losses or a Himalaya of gains. Though Bernt's reputation extended beyond the frontiers of

Sweden, he had been reduced to accepting with grati-
tude the company of a stranger, a young writer and
lecturer who was a guest of the cultural circle in
Kiruna. Who else could have listened to him with
such patience? At the end of two days of anguished
reflection, it was consoling to have at his side another
human being, to be comforted by his presence. How
was he to forget Nils's voice saying: "Frankly, Bernt,
I haven't the slightest feeling of responsibility, reci-
procity or attachment for you. You were brought up
by someone else." With those words, Bernt's entire
world had crumbled. He had not known that an adult
could retain a child's unlimited capacity to suffer.

As for religion, Luther's principles had left him
with reservations. The initiation had been long, the
texts demanding, the discipline austere. At his examination on graduating from high school, he had received the highest marks in his class, but he had by
then ceased to believe in the Church's teachings. As
an adult, he went to church as one fulfills a social
obligation, to prove to his children and to the community at large that he was not an atheist but a high-
minded citizen. The meaning of the services he
attended escaped him. His spiritual wellspring had
gone dry. As he stood with his family and listened to
the psalms being sung, Bernt had been irritated to
find himself bowing to a constraint which was part
and parcel of the established order. But the president
of the Group was required to set an example. And
what good had that done him? Now, at the decisive
hour of his life, he found himself without a pastor,
without any other confidant than this stranger sent to
him by chance.

He had hesitated to discuss with Pierre the changes

that would take place in the highest echelon of the
Group. The novelist knew nothing about the world of
business. A Swedish conglomerate would make no
sense to him; the president of a company with mul-
tinational ramifications would in his eyes be like a
specimen of an unknown species to be contemplated
with the detachment of a zoologist. Unconsciously,
Bernt had hoped that his guest would deliver him
from the torment which had destroyed within him
even his desire to be saved. The scene with Nils still
rankled. He had been rejected, stripped of his insig-
nia. Had he the courage to go on without hope of
winning back his lost crown and scepter? Ulla might
have understood him, stood by him, sustained him.
But she had given him only her body. Bernt remained
alone facing the all-powerful Lena, who had arisen
from the depths of the night, escaped from the sub-
terranean kingdom of Hel, guardian of those who die
far from the battlefield.

Why had the gods not sent him Ulla instead of this
nice but ineffectual Frenchman? He thirsted for Ulla,
the embodiment of love and life. She would have
healed his wounds, stanched the hemorrhage through
which his strength was ebbing. Only a woman can repair the havoc wrought by another woman.

He was doomed to walk an arid path, with this
stranger as his sole companion. Pierre was not holding
out his hand to this man sinking into the mire, but
was instead passionately interested in the Scandinavian legends. He asked questions about Odin, master
of all the gods, the magician who can turn himself
into a bird or a reindeer, who calms the sea and
makes the winds blow, who metes out death or misfortune, cleaves open rocks and burial mounds, pene-

trates matter whether it be living or inanimate. All science comes from Odin, who is also the god of weaponry. Those who succumb in battle are Odin's sons whom he gathers home to his sacred Valhalla, set in a grove of trees bearing golden fruits, a palatial hall with its five hundred portals, each of which can admit eight hundred men walking abreast. Before choosing among them, the lord and master of the gods (with Thor, the god of thunder, at his side) marks them with his sign—a gash on the face. For the man who receives this stigma there exists no further limit nor hour. In the great hall hung with trophies, Odin and his companions drink mead served by the Walkyries, and in the inner gardens fight battles in which they are never wounded. Odin's sons are delivered from the thirst to live, from the taste for riches, from desire and from greed; they are heroes who have attained perfect joy.

Pierre was curious about the Book: "In the beginning nothing existed, neither waves, nor the earth, nor the skies. The abysses opened, no grass grew . . ." First there was the Ginnungagap, a gulf at the bottom of which flowed a river, imprisoned by ice. The northern frost had met the wind from the south which, by licking the ice, had freed Ymir, father of the giants of the frost, and Aumdula the cow, as well as Buri, whose son Bor had given birth to Odin and his two brothers who ruled the universe. After having ordained day, night, and the seasons, from an ash tree and an elm washed up on the shore they redeemed the first man and the first woman—Ask and Embla.

What use was it to hope for a miracle? He might as well go along with this courteous young man who was finding amusement in his unusual evening. Bernt explained Scandinavian mythology, then remarked: "I haven't read your books. What are they about?"

"The novel I'm writing now is about the myth of the double. Roger is a novelist who has been twice divorced and who goes to the United States on a lecture tour. At the same time, he is running away from a love affair that he finds oppressive. In New York he meets a young industrialist, heir to a wood manufacturer, who tells him about the most modern methods of laminating wood. Ordinarily these two men would have nothing in common. However, the writer is attracted to his tranquil companion and sees in him himself as he might have been if his life had taken a different turning. John represents one of his possible destinies. His house by a river, through whose windows drift the sound of bees and the perfume of linden trees, his wife who makes jam and wears decorous nightgowns, fascinate Roger the jet-setter. His host's childhood seems to him to have been his own, this house whose terrace overlooks the valley in a peaceful town his own house. He and John have had similar mothers. If he, Roger, had not chosen another card from the deck which Fate had held out to him, he might have been a man like his host. By a kind of spiritual breaking and entering he penetrates into the industrialist's private life, his inner being."

"But how do you know about all this?"

"A novelist has the ability to put himself in another's place. When I write about my characters, I forget who I am."

"And do you exercise this same talent in real life?"

Pierre considered the question.

"Let's see now. You're an important businessman. Your being here in the middle of the week is out of the ordinary. I don't believe that a woman could have made you put aside your responsibilities to come here on a Wednesday. The forest is the Swedes' womb; no doubt you're looking for the answer to a problem having to do with your balance sheets or your percentages."

Bernt made no comment. He was so tired! It was too late. The hour when he might have turned back had passed.

Pierre hesitated. Should he risk being indiscreet? The man before him appeared to be exhausted: His eyes were deeply circled, his features were drawn, his expression haggard. Pierre felt that he could not presume to pry into what was causing him such obvious pain. Could the problem be concerned solely with money? The novelist detested the breed of profit-obsessed men who dreamed only of capital, of amassing wealth, and whose hearts beat in rhythm with the stock-exchange tickers. Bernt seemed to him to be different from the financiers he had seen on television, who hardly differed from the old nineteenth-century robber barons—save that they lacked the latter's imagination and force. "A business concern is a contract set up with a view to profits," he had heard one of them say. "It is unthinkable to submit the execution of such a contract to the evaluation and control of third parties who are alien to it." By "third parties" he had meant his workers, even his executive staff.

Pierre told Bernt that he believed a business represented not only the goods produced but also an ensemble of human beings, a collectivity to which the employer bore a responsibility. In his view, the man who exercised the power of running a business without taking into account the best interests of his employees should, in the event of a misfortune in which those employees suffered, be held responsible.

Bernt protested.

"That doesn't apply to us. It's usually not our employees who give us trouble, but our partners."

He made a gesture as if he were brushing away an insect.

"I'd rather hear about the rest of your novel. What happens to your character in the United States?"

Pierre realized that he had touched a nerve. Before operating to remove a tumor, the doctor must obtain the patient's consent. As soon as he had approached the danger zone, Bernt had hastened to change the subject. Better to stick to literature.

"John must make a trip to Savannah, and Roger accompanies him. I shall describe the shadowy old houses; the perfume of magnolias and jasmine; the sun-dappled streets, the cries of the fruit-sellers; the oaks, cypresses and cedars; the swamps covered with birds; the red earth of the South that reeked during the War Between the States with the blood of a hundred thousand twenty-year-old boys. Roger's concern is how to get rid of the possessive woman he has left behind in Paris."

Bernt smiled.

"May I give you some advice? Let's pretend that you and I are traveling in the same compartment of a train and that I'm about to get off; after all, we shall undoubtedly never meet again. Get into the habit of being with young people. Organize a roundtable of students on television. Invite them to your house. You will let some fresh air into your mind and you will meet a young girl. I won't presume to go any further. Would you like a beer?"

"No, thank you. What time is it? Ten past four! You've brought me back to my youthful discussions about society, progress, the future, the meaning of life. How far are we from my hotel? I ought to get some sleep—otherwise the people of Kiruna will be disappointed in me."

Bernt rose to his feet. He had once again donned his civilized mask.

"If you prefer to return to town, I'll take you. We're in the forest preserve here, on the other side of the mines. It's only about twenty kilometers."

The last guest was leaving, the mission unaccomplished. How could Pierre have known that he had been chatting with a man in dire peril? If he had come upon Bernt in the act of drowning himself, Pierre would have plunged in to save him. But this civil man in a monogrammed shirt and flannel trousers, reclining gracefully on his bed with his arms folded under his head, did not inspire pity.

Bernt wondered if he should call Ulla. He had hardly had the time to love her. She would probably answer that her husband was back from his trip, that she was not free, that her father required her presence. If they had continued to meet secretly, they would have been obliged to steal time from Bernt's business, from Ingrid, from the shipbuilder; they would have been forced to invent pretexts to meet on weekends; they would have learned to greet each other indifferently in the presence of their friends. A love that is dissimulated is called an "affair," and affairs are made to be broken. Too many obstacles would have separated him from Ulla.

Bernt tied his necktie, put on his jacket, and led the way downstairs under the staring eyes of the wolves with their grinning fangs. The Bentley turned into the Jukkasjärvi forest road. In the moonlight the conifers seemed to possess a strange life of their own. Of what use was it to invoke Freya—the friend of lovers who, with Odin, reigns over the dead and who drives a chariot drawn by two cats—to ask her to bring Ulla to him? The gods were silent, not because they were dead but because men had forgotten how to speak their language. The incantations had been discarded, the rites abolished.

As he drove, Bernt told Pierre about the nocturnal horse that sprinkles the earth with dew each morning.

"The past still holds us in its spell. We believe in our legends because we need to appease the invisible powers. Tomorrow, piles of faggots will be lighted on the hills to celebrate the first of May and the return of the sun goddess."

Pierre was sorry not to have visited the Lapp museum at Jukkasjärvi, where he would have seen the stones of the altar.

"They are ancient dolmens. Human sacrifices to the great goddess were once offered on them. You saw one of them in the clearing under the oak tree."

"I have so little time! At noon the members of the cultural association will come to take me to a magnificent smorgasbord. Afterward I'll give my talk, and at four o'clock my plane leaves for Stockholm."

The automobile entered the outskirts of the newly constructed city of Kiruna. In the town's center rose a church in the form of a Lapp tent. Frost gleamed along the crests of the housetops. Pierre realized that the end of the trip was at hand, and took out a notebook from his pocket to write down his name and address for Bernt in case he came to Paris. The car stopped; the two men shook hands. Bernt drove away without a backward glance.

He left the highway and entered the forest. The midnight sun would be visible from the end of May to the fifteenth of July. The car left shallow ruts in the newly fallen snow. An unreal light bathed the forest. Bernt should have caught the first plane to Stockholm at five o'clock in the morning to meet with his lawyer and prepare the conditions of his resignation under the most honorable terms. Since he would no longer be playing a role in the family business, nothing could prevent him from finding interesting work with one of the Group's competitors. But he could no more imagine himself stealing markets from the Group than he could see himself taking orders from Carl. There remained the possibility of exile. New York tempted him. In that city, compared to which the rest of the world is a province, careers could be made on a planetary scale. He would have been happy there with a terrace at the top of a skyscraper, Wall Street, dynamic friends. The dream rang false. Bernt knew that he was too attached to the Group to work anywhere else.

If Lena had lived, he would have laid his head on her lap without having to explain himself. She would have advised him tenderly. In time of trial, the maternal fortress is a haven of security, peace, comfort; he would have found shelter in full measure. Instead, he was fated to struggle alone.

He parked the Bentley in the garage. His mind was functioning with extraordinary precision. Sleep? What for? A twenty-minute walk away, via the shortcut, Lena awaited him in the clearing. He went to the gun rack where Lars's weapons were displayed in pairs, took down a Purdey with a stock of engine-turned silver, tried the hammer, took off the safety catch, shoved several cartridges into his trouser pocket, and put the weapon in two sections into its leather case.

As he hurried toward his rendezvous, the new-fallen snow crackled under his boots. Between the reddish trunks of the fir trees a ribbon of moonlight pointed the way to Lena.

XIV

He approached the clearing, the gun case slung over his shoulder, setting one foot before the other like an automaton, weariness dragging at his every step. His mind was like a broken kaleidoscope, its images dissolved into a nebulous, formless mass. Bits of landscape, vague impressions flooded in, helter-skelter, upon the screen of his memory: Now he saw the sea at Storö with breakers crashing down on the sand, now the nape of Donatella's neck, now the New York that he had enjoyed; then the strong taste of certain victories, the frustration of Lena's absence. His emotions changed from one instant to the next, depending on the scene or the association of ideas. In June, even in Sweden, at noon a heat haze like that which veils the hills of Siena causes shadows to vibrate like blue embers; when he remembered that, Donatella was restored to him. In the same way, a recollected sound, an intonation, brought to life the Birgit of his youth, her pigtails, her sweet intensity. Despite the passing of the years, each moment of passion flowered in him anew, its thrills intact, victorious over the erosion of time.

Bernt controlled his breathing, spared his gestures; exhaustion was seeping into his marrow. Not a shiver, not a murmur, not a whisper animated the trees, frozen in wait for the moment when they might reach for light and sun. Suddenly a flight of cranes swept across the sky. The sound of their passing was followed, like an echo, by the barking of staghounds far away in the forest. Odin's hunt! Bernt repressed a shudder. A twig whipped across his face and he recoiled. The spot on his forehead burned. He raised a finger to the place and brought it away covered with blood.

A faint glimmer filtered through the forest. The growing rays of light told him that his goal was close at hand. Under the giant oak with its mighty branches the dolmen waited, eternity beckoned to him. As he approached the stone, a sensation of great relief came to him. The ash trees, the firs, and the birches had been awaiting him in this clearing since the hour of his birth.

Bernt laid down the Purdey, still encased in its leather sheath bearing Lars's monogram, among the roots which, before burying themselves in the earth, spread out from the great oak's trunk like the fingers of a giant hand.

He dusted the snow from the dolmen and sat down on the slab. He felt detached, as though he had entered a physical state of suspended animation while his spirit wandered elsewhere. His father's hatred,

Carl's revenge, the murmurs of envy that he could still hear, but faintly as if on the other side of an invisible, protecting wall, no longer touched him.

Little by little the trees around him let fall their robes of bark, which are designed to lead the uninitiated astray, and appeared dressed as warriors leaning on the handles of their heavy swords. Some wore helmets and masks and bore lances and wheel-shaped bucklers, in the centers of which blossomed suns with spiral rays. Booted, wearing their halberdiers' tunics, they stood immobile, awaiting the start of the ceremony that would admit him to their clan. Bernt realized that the children had fled on tiptoe; that Ulla and Ingrid had departed; that Otto, Erik, Albert, Bo, and Jan had taken to their heels along with Nils, Carl, and the prime minister. The last boundary had been crossed.

The cold pierced through his fur-lined raincoat; dampness seeped into his bones. Trembling, he leapt up and paced back and forth in the clearing, under the steady scrutiny of the watching giants. What did it matter if they were impatient! Bernt was in no hurry. His hour would arrive soon enough. He was like a traveler in space contemplating his former planet, a blue sphere suspended in the universe. How could he have allowed himself to become so immersed in mundane events? What sense had there been in all that hurly-burly? His consuming interest—his religion, his faith—had been the development of the Group. How was it possible that he had cared so much about winning or losing! The Group would survive without him. His name would crop up in a reassuring conversational formula: "Poor Bernt, he was obviously suffering from nervous depression. He

wasn't a terribly well-balanced young man after all."
"He lacked the stamina to take on such heavy responsibilities," others would say. In lowered voices, some
members of his staff would recall a scene just before
his death when he and his uncle had disagreed about
a tanker option. Finally, silence would settle over his
memory, as implacably as flakes of snow cover the
tracks of a fox. It would be easy enough to make up
false explanations, to avoid laying the blame for his
death where it really belonged. His father and his
uncle would live out their lives in an atmosphere of
universal respect, reaping all the honors due their fortunes and their rank. Who does not respect power allied to wealth? Ingrid (who would undoubtedly
remarry within three years) would make a perfect
widow; Nils, Carl, and their families would look
properly solemn in their mourning clothes. At the
thought of Lars, Viveca, and Axel, Bernt's eyes filled
with tears.

And Lena? She had contributed to his downfall, for
the child requires absolutely that his mother corre-
spond to the image of her that he has created. He
seemed to hear her calling his name, her voice
echoing under the vast vault of the trees. "Not yet!"
he cried.

He was gasping. He knelt by the gun case, unfas-
tened the buckle that held down the leather cover,
took out the stock, wrapped in brown canvas tied
with a lace. A scent of sandalwood arose from it. The
stock had the satin texture of a baby's skin; he drew
its lovely shape across his palm with sensuous
pleasure. Near the trigger, the grained wood was
shaped in the form of a double diamond; on the silver
plates edging the safety lock, an artist had carved a

garland of those full-petaled hollyhocks which lend
the English countryside their simple charm; on each
side of the break of the barrel was a silver sunflower
enclosed in delicate arabesques, in their center the
signature—"Purdey's patent"; under the small of the
butt, between screws in the form of the sun, was
printed the number—"19431." The weapon he was ex-
amining in such minute detail gave him a feeling of
security, engendering, without eliminating temptation, its own prophylaxis in the form of an esthetic
delight. Bernt had been trapped remorselessly; even
now his family believed him to be wandering within
a labyrinth, searching for a way out of the maze. But
he knew a way out, a way that would help him to escape the hell devised for him by his own people! The
tension of these last days had been too great; he had
no strength left to endure the agony.

This weapon was his last friend, the ultimate
presence with whose help he would burst his bonds,
escape from the inextricable. Whose finger would
really pull the trigger? Lars had seduced Bernt's
mother, and by doing so had deprived her of the serenity of an ordinary existence. Carl had denounced
his sister-in-law's conduct and had given her over to
the vengeance of Nils, the self-appointed instrument
of fate. First Nils had rejected the mother, then the
son, with words that still rang in Bernt's ears. Lena,
the agent of this misfortune, now opened her arms to
Bernt, calling to him in a voice he had never heard
before.

The mouths of the gun's barrels resembled empty
eye-sockets—blind death, the unseeing look of the
dead. He lay the two sections of his gun on the altar.
Perhaps he was planning to kill himself for the wrong

reason! Why should he renounce his prerogatives? Because he was fatigued beyond measure and had no more desire to struggle. He wished to know only the inert peace of a stone, like those recumbent figures carved on tombs. He wanted only to stretch out and never get up again, to lie on a bed of snow, lulled, at peace. Strangers might handle his body, might profane his mortal shell, but that would not matter. Then a luminous memory came to him. Several years before, when a helicopter service had functioned between the Pan American Building and Kennedy Airport, he had flown over New York at seven o'clock in the evening. Brilliant scarves of orange and gold light had set the glittering surface of the Hudson River on fire. Since he had decided against exile in the United States, today he would fly off to an unknown destination.

Bernt took the stock in his left hand, the barrels in his right. Usually he assembled his gun swiftly and mechanically, but this time he made several tries without success. Would he be obliged to return to the lodge to check the gun's mate, hanging on the rack in the living room? He knew that he would never be able to return to the clearing a second time. Suicide is a divine gift which one must know how to seize at the perfect moment. His hands trembled.

His heart was beating so loudly that he could hear it echoing through the forest. The trees regarded him steadily. He sank down on the dolmen and closed his eyes. An oppression was weighing on his chest, slowly suffocating him. When the pain subsided, he perceived once more the attentive warriors standing in the clearing bathed in moonlight. Again he seized the stock and the barrels, and this time he succeeded in securing the hooks. He threw the bolt and the gun was ready. All that remained was to load it. One cartridge and it would be done.

Suddenly he saw a young woman, her blond hair flowing loose, the folds of her long white gown floating on the air, walking lightly towards him. Lena! Barefoot, smiling, a finger on her lips, the apparition entered the clearing. Bernt leaned for support against the giant oak. Lena came to him, caressed his forehead and smiled gently. He felt the sting of a razor cut; her periwinkle-blue nails were colder than ice.

Her words, barely a murmur, were scarcely audible.

"Come, my son. It's been so long! Come, my darling. I'll rock you, I'll sing you songs, I'll never leave you again."

A bird, sitting on the branch of a birch tree, began its trill. Dawn had come.

Lena's voice was like a whispery breath.

"O Bernt, come to me, my little one! Don't leave me!"

With a rustling of feathers, a woodcock flew up and away. Lena sighed.

"Good-bye, Bernt. Farewell, my son."

He could not allow her to return alone to the kingdom of the dead. She was beginning to vanish, to melt into the mists of the dawning day, to disintegrate into winking opalescent reflections.

"Wait! I'm coming! Wait for me!" he cried.

She was the beginning of the world; she alone possessed the power to return him to a lost paradise.

Just then the warriors, in obedience to a mysterious order, advanced toward him, sword in hand.

XV

FIVE O'CLOCK SOUNDED FROM THE CHURCH STEEPLE IN
Kiruna. Pierre had been in bed trying to sleep for the
past half hour, but he had not closed his eyes. Was
his insomnia due to being in a foreign land so near to
the polar circle? During his recent adventure, he had
crossed into a forbidden latitude, had entered a
topsy-turvy place where the laws were different from
those he understood. An uneasiness remained with
him, a growing regret. Bernt had been kind to him,
had treated him like a brother. Had he received in return what he had hoped for? Perhaps he had stopped
short of telling Pierre his innermost thoughts because
Pierre had not known how to inspire his confidence.
"Pretend that you and I are traveling in the same
compartment of a train and that I am about to get off
. . ." He should have led Bernt to confess to what
was on his mind. Instead of which, Pierre had been

content to describe ,his novel and had happily accepted advice concerning his own private life. His encounter with an industrialist accustomed to weighing both sides of an argument and then making a choice had made a deep impression on him. Bernt had been right, his advice excellent. As soon as he got back to Paris, Pierre intended to see less of Leonore. He planned to be honest with her, to tell her that he was in no position to assure her future. Once free of that relationship, he would invite young people, students, to his home, and his life would be enriched.

He remained awake, oppressed by a sense of foreboding. His window was closed, the heating system was functioning normally, the hotel seemed peaceful. Nothing was threatening him. He forced himself to go over the early part of the evening in order to distract his thoughts from the presentiment of danger that he felt stealing over him. The Selsvikens had been friendly. Almost everyone had read his novels. They owned copies translated into Swedish and had discussed them with him, their perceptions interesting and to the point. Ordinarily Pierre was astonished at the subtle intentions ascribed to him by French critics. He wrote only of what came to him from his imagination. At the age of ten, he had told himself stories before going to sleep at night, and the next day he had transcribed them into notebooks. There were boxes of those notebooks, filled with a schoolboy's scrawl, in his grandparents' attic.

His thoughts wandered. He would also invite some television journalists for dinner. He might marry; an intelligent young wife would draw him out of his shell. He would move away from the rue Mazarine to a larger, sunnier apartment, would write more articles, participate on literary juries, become a truly active member of the Parisian literary world.

These reveries did not succeed in calming him. He was afraid! His throat was knotted with apprehension, there was a cramp in his stomach, his hands and feet were icy cold, his scalp prickled, his heart fluttered. Should he have a drink? He should have brought some sleeping pills with him, though he had never needed to resort to them before. Was he about to have a heart attack? Was he doomed to suffer until morning? He couldn't possibly call for room service until seven o'clock. Two hours to wait. He would ask for the name and address of a doctor. Perhaps Bernt could tell him of one. He had noted the number written in the center of Bernt's telephone dial. Should he call him at such an ungodly hour? He must have returned to the lodge and gone to bed. Well, he would try him just the same, and ask for the name of a good cardiologist.

Pierre rang Bernt's number. The ringing went on and on. Was Bernt asleep? The phone was by his bed. What could he be doing? Pierre hung up. Could Bernt have a mistress living nearby? Not likely, or he wouldn't have welcomed a stranger so readily. What could he be doing at this hour? The roads were covered with snow, the cafés closed, the countryside paralyzed by the cold. Where was he?

Pierre called again. The ringing went on interminably. Could he be with friends? Not at five o'clock in the morning! He turned out the light and forced himself to lie perfectly still, his arms at his sides. His heartbeat grew steady, his mind emptied itself of agonizing hypotheses. A vision of Bernt came to him—an accident, why hadn't he thought of that? He might have missed a turn, might be lying in a ditch. Had he struck a tree? The certainty grew in him that Bernt was in danger.

Pierre did not believe in telepathy, but he observed that his tenseness and apprehension had left him as soon as he had begun to think of Bernt. Had Bernt called out to him for help? He searched for the telephone book and called for a taxi. In mangled English with a few words of German thrown in, Pierre managed to make himself understood. He dressed hurriedly, dashed downstairs and out the door. The street was deserted, no automobile was in sight. He stamped his feet on the pavement to warm them. What had come over him to make him undertake this adventure? Bernt would laugh when he learned how he had raced to help him. At the street corner the beam of a pair of headlights pierced the gloom. A black automobile stopped in front of him, and a young man rolled down the window and leaned out.

"Did you call me?" he asked.

Pierre opened the door and got into the back seat, nodding affirmatively.

He explained that he had just telephoned to a friend, the owner of a stone shooting lodge in the forest preserve, with whom he had spent the evening. The driver's expression changed.

"Ah! I know who you mean. A very important man."

Pierre said that he was afraid his friend might have met with an accident, since his phone did not answer. Was it possible to go there to see if the gentleman was all right? he inquired.

Rubbing imaginary banknotes between his fingers,

the driver asked: "*Ar det langt hari fran? Far? Hur mycket?* How much?"

"Whatever you say. But hurry! Hurry!"

The driver started the car. Soon the houses grew sparse and the forest reigned supreme. He slowed down at a crossroads and asked Pierre whether they should turn right or left, but the Frenchman could not remember. The young man shook his head, stopped the car, took a map from the glove compartment and began to study it. Then he shrugged, put the vehicle in gear and turned east, into the forest. Pierre reproached himself for not having paid attention to the road, when he had taken it with Bernt. What in the name of heaven had come over him? It would have been more intelligent to have stayed in his warm room at the hotel, instead of waking Bernt out of a sound sleep.

By a miracle the car stopped before the huge stone cube. The windows were dark, blank.

"Wait here."

Pierre pressed the bell. There was no answer. Should he break a window? He succeeded in finding one unlocked, and opened it. Immediately the driver broke into a vehement flood of Swedish. Pierre interrupted his tirade.

"Please, please! Come in with me. He may be sick!"

Inside, he turned on the lights. It seemed strange to be there without Bernt, in the room in which they had eaten supper, to see the dead fire, the overturned bottles of beer. The kitchen, like the dining room, was empty. As he was about to go upstairs, followed by the grumbling driver, Pierre stopped short. He had noted the absence of the Purdey on the rack. He took the stairs four at a time and flung open the door to the bedroom. The room was still in the state in which he had last seen it. A hollow showed on the bed where Bernt's long body had stretched out. Nothing had been disturbed. He was losing precious time! Where could one hunt at such an hour?—and without dogs!

A pang shot through him. What reason would a man have for taking a walk at five in the morning carrying a gun? Where would he go? Pierre descended the stairs slowly, followed by the taxi driver, who stared curiously at the mounted heads of the reindeer and wolves. Bernt's voice echoed in Pierre's memory: "On the night of the great thaw, each person discovers his own truth. The cards are reshuffled, everyone receives a new hand." He had shown him the sacrificial stone. "Look at that dolmen. Only animals come here now. You and I are the first pilgrims in several thousand years." Suddenly Pierre understood. They must find the clearing as quickly as possible. He seized the driver by his coat collar and told him that they must look for an oak tree and an ancient altar, then he asked if he had a large-scale map of the forest preserve.

The Swede glared at him stubbornly. He was going back to Kiruna, he declared. He refused to be trotted around in the woods at such an ungodly hour by a crazy foreigner, he shouted.

"Please! I'll pay you anything you ask. Anything!" Pierre begged.

Still glowering, the taxi driver answered him in English, with the guttural accent of the northern woodcutters.

"Go on your own. If you want to walk in the woods at this hour, I won't stop you. But I'm leaving!"

For the first time in many years Pierre uttered a silent prayer, asking God to grant him the power to convince this man to help him.

"I'm not imagining things, my friend. The important man who lives in this house has left here alone, carrying a gun with him. I'm afraid for his safety. He and I spent the evening together. He talked a lot; he was uneasy, unhappy. At the time, I didn't understand how much he needed me! Take me to him, please! We can't leave him alone. We're wasting precious minutes standing here arguing like this!"

With a shrug, the young man agreed to come. He took out a map and, after a few moments of study, pointed out a paler area within the green mass of the preserve, in the center of which was a minuscule circle.

While the driver kept his foot on the gas pedal, speeding down the road, Pierre prayed like a child that Bernt would be all right, that they would get to him in time.

The driver turned around in his seat, indicating with a gesture of his arm a narrow path leading away from the road into the forest. They left the car and continued on foot, tramping over the snow among the fir trees, which had taken on the appearance of cathedrals with dark spires. The crack of a branch broken by their passing, the sound of rushing water, the plaintive cries of a screech owl punctuated the eerie silence.

Pierre had the impression that he had lived through these moments once before, that on some previous journey he had traveled through these jungle-thick woods where no light filtered, had felt this terrible sensation of deadly exhaustion. He mastered his fa-

tigue and concentrated upon his objective—to arrive
in time to save Bernt, to comfort him and stay with
him. They would talk with utter frankness this time,
would bare their hearts. Pierre planned to suggest
that Bernt come to Paris and stay with him until he
was fit to return to work in Stockholm. If he didn't arrive in time, if . . . he tried to drive the horrible
spectre from his thoughts . . . a day would not pass
on which he would not castigate himself for having
been so blind. Nonassistance to a person in danger,
that had been his crime. He would be the last person
to have seen Bernt, to have shared his thoughts during the last three hours of his life. Pierre shuddered
and hurried on.

The driver touched his sleeve. Between the
branches an opening showed among the great trees.
Beams of moonlight illuminated an oak tree, which
Pierre recognized. They had arrived at their destination.

Bernt lay stretched at the foot of the dolmen, his
head reposing in a pool of blood that had been absorbed by the snow. His face had not been damaged.
Open-eyed, smiling, he was staring over the tops of
the birches toward a patch of luminescence, shaped
like a halo, in the sky. Dawn was breaking.

ALL TIME BESTSELLERS
FROM POPULAR LIBRARY

Dorothy Dunnett

THE LYMOND CHRONICLE

THE GREATEST HISTORICAL SAGA OF OUR AGE BY A WRITER "AS GOOD AS MARY RENAULT" (*Sunday Times*, London), "AS POPULAR AS TOLKIEN" (Cleveland Magazine), WHO "COULD TEACH SCHEHERAZADE A THING OR TWO ABOUT SUSPENSE, PACE AND INVENTION" (*New York Times*), AND WHO IS "ONE OF THE GREATEST TALE-SPINNERS SINCE DUMAS" (*Cleveland Plain Dealer*).

☐ THE GAME OF KINGS	08571-1	1.95
☐ QUEENS' PLAY	08496-0	1.95
☐ THE DISORDERLY KNIGHTS	08497-9	1.95
☐ PAWN IN FRANKINCENSE	08472-3	1.95
☐ THE RINGED CASTLE	08495-2	1.95
☐ CHECKMATE	08483-9	1.95

Buy them at your local bookstores or use this handy coupon for ordering:

Green Thumb
Answers To
House Plant Questions

Everything the indoor gardener needs to know about house plants, with easy-to-follow instructions for their care, problems and propagation

☐ BRINGING THE OUTDOORS IN—Loewer	08471-5	1.95
☐ BRINGING THE OUTDOORS IN—Loewer (8 x 11)	08464-2	4.95
☐ THE COMPLETE BOOK OF GARDENING UNDER LIGHTS—McDonald	03014-3	1.50
☐ DON'T SWALLOW THE AVOCADO PIT & WHAT TO DO WITH THE REST OF IT —Rosenbaum	03072-0	1.50
☐ THE HOUSE PLANT ANSWER BOOK —McDonald	03078-X	1.50
☐ HOUSE PLANTS TO GROW IF YOU HAVE NO SUN—McDonald	03082-8	1.50
☐ HOW TO BUILD YOUR OWN GREENHOUSE—McDonald	03140-9	1.50
☐ HOW TO GROW HERBS AND SALAD GREENS INDOORS—Meschter	03043-7	1.50
☐ THE INDOOR WATER GARDENER'S HOW-TO-HANDBOOK—Loewer	08270-4	1.25
☐ INTRODUCTION TO TERRARIUMS —Grubman	08488-X	1.50
☐ LITTLE PLANTS FOR SMALL SPACES —McDonald	03035-6	1.50
☐ THE MONTH BY MONTH GUIDE TO INDOOR GARDENING—Druse	04023-8	1.50
☐ NEVER-SAY-DIE HOUSE PLANTS —McDonald	08524-X	1.50
☐ SEEDS AND CUTTINGS—Loewer	03184-0	1.50
☐ THE WORLD BOOK OF HOUSE PLANTS—McDonald (8 x 11)	08510-X	4.95
☐ THE WORLD BOOK OF HOUSE PLANTS—McDonald	03152-2	1.50

Buy them at your local bookstores or use this handy coupon for ordering:

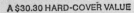